For the
DURATION

Nancy
Cathers
Phillips

Library of Congress Control Number: 2018963939
ISBN-13: 978-0-9968819-7-5
ISBN-10: 0-9968819-7-2

Penstemon
Publications
Wellington, CO 80549

www.penstemonpublications.com

Foreword

Nancy Cathers Phillips: Oct. 14, 1935 – Nov. 1, 2016

Nancy Cathers was a young girl during World War II, growing up in a small town in New Jersey. A family with a German surname lived in a house across the street from her, with a boy about her age named Carl. One night the family disappeared, and rumors circulated around the town that they were Nazi spies. For the rest of her life Nancy wondered what happened to Carl and his family, but she never found out. Later on in life she began to do some research on the arrest and internment of Americans of German ancestry, along with Japanese-Americans. At one point she came in contact with a man, born in America, who had been interned with his parents. He in fact was also sent to a prison in Germany as a boy of twelve, after the war. He has written a book about his experience (*The Prison Called Hohenasperg,* by Arthur D. Jacobs). Among my memories is a visit with Nancy to Ellis Island, where some German-Americans were interned during the war.

In recent years Nancy decided to write a story about a German-American boy, named Carl, who was arrested, along with his family, and sent to an internment camp during World War II. The story is also about his friendship with his neighbor Claire, a girl about his age, and their efforts to find each other after the war. While the story is fiction, it is based on actual history. While writing this story, Nancy was a member of a writing group, from whom she got critiques and encouragement. This same group has provided valuable help in getting this story published posthumously. I am grateful to the members of this group, including Judie Freeland, Clare Rutherford, Mim Neal, Susan Quinlan, Gary Raham, Libby James, Nancy Burns, Bev Hadden, and Linda White. They have been longtime friends to Nancy, and I consider them my friends now. I am especially grateful to Linda White, a writing buddy to Nancy for over twenty years. She assembled all the computer files left by Nancy into a publishable novel. And also to Gary Raham, who designed the book cover and did all the mechanics of getting the book published.

Wayne Phillips, in memory of my life partner

Nancy Cathers Phillips

There is no agony like bearing an untold story inside you.
Zora Neale Hurston

Summer, 2007

Chapter
1

I sit in the window seat at the front of the second floor hall, look-ing through the green treetops toward Stone Pond and wonder what in heaven's name I will do with all this stuff. The time has come to move on, or at least to start getting ready to move on, but the mere thought of dealing with fifty years' accumulation stag-gers me.

We used to joke, Link and I, about leaving with a duffel bag of clothes apiece and a sack full of favorite books and tossing a lighted match behind us as we cleared the front sill. Of course we would never destroy this beautiful, rambling old house where we raised our two plus Richard's one, and where the ghosts of half a dozen dogs and too many cats to count lurk in doorways ready to pounce on one another. Link will not be leaving when I go.

Ringo, the last of the border collies, still hangs in there, but we're both getting on. I'll turn seventy-four this November. Ringo's nine and a half, sixty-something in dog years. We've kept in good shape hiking these New Hampshire woods, but the years begin to weigh us down. And without Link, I am an amputee.

Mother, in an assisted living facility near the New Jersey shore, is too far away for me to make regular visits. We have some unfin-ished business, oddly enough, and I, like a lot of older people, find myself drawn back to the town where I grew up. We spent the war years in Marlsburg. I learned to run a household and had my first marriage proposal at age eight and a half. I still wonder about my friend Carl and his parents after all these years. Where did they go? And why?

When the phone rings, I get up and walk toward my bedroom,

avoiding the purple and blue throw rug I should probably get rid of, but which Laurel made in Girl Scouts and I'm not ready to part with. Ringo gets up slowly and, pressed against my leg, accompanies me. It's Phoebe, my only granddaughter.

"Grandmother." Her voice has a lovely lilt to it, but I sense some buttering-up. She wants something. I am likely to give it.

"Granddaughter." Ringo nudges me to pet him. With my hand on his warm head I smile and wait for her to tell me why she is calling.

"Okay. I had this thought."

"Okay. You have a lot of thoughts."

"Yes, but this is one of my best. You see, I really really need to get out of Colorado for a while. Like this whole school year?" she says in a rush.

"Trouble in paradise?"

"Sean, the scumbag, dumped me."

Oh, frabjous day, I think, but of course don't say it. "What a foolish young man he is," is what I do say.

"He's a turd."

I would never have gotten away with saying that when I was young if I had even known the term. Had I? Probably not. It was the Age of Euphemisms. I remember that back in the early forties Petey Merino's sister was decked by her mother for saying 'pregnant.' "So, what's the rest of the thought, Phoebe Bird?"

"I could, um, transfer to Lyndon College, and live with you? Be a townie? Mom says you're planning to clear out the house. I could help lug stuff. We could sell things on eBay, or have a yard sale, or whatever. And we could talk." A long pause ensues. "Please, Gran?" This time I hear the tears in her voice and my heart says "yes, oh, yes."

"If it's okay with your parents, I'd love nothing better than to have a year with you."

"They're all for it. I think I'm driving them nuts."

"What are kids for?" We laugh and already I am envisioning the wonderful year ahead, hikes in the woods with Ringo, snowshoeing, fires in the fireplace, a weekend on the Maine coast, making a quilt together, Christmas. "When would you come?"

"Like...Monday?"

This is Saturday. I don't have anything planned I can't get out of except the Historical Society tea here tomorrow. "Would I be right in supposing you already have your ticket?"

"Well, yeah."

I laugh again. "You're pretty sure of yourself, Miss Phoebe."

"I'm pretty sure of you," she says.

Who could resist such loving blandishments? For the first time since Link's death I feel a glimmer of joy. "What time do you get in?"

She tells me. I write the time and the flight number on the pad I keep on my bedside table, and, after we hang up, begin a list.

Chapter 2

❝I can't believe you still have this," Phoebe exclaims, a smile growing on her face. She holds up a painting she did in first grade, of an elephant standing in tall green grass. Laurel had it framed and mailed it to Link and me. We both loved the picture, for its clear, strong colors and goofy humor. The elephant appears to be doing a jig.

"It's a wonderful picture, Phoeb."

"For someone with no discernible talent for painting," she says.

"Well, perhaps it was an anomaly, but it's still a wonderful picture. Grandpa and I smiled every time we looked at it."

"You're such a grandma," she says, pleased.

We are in the attic, wearing jeans and sweatshirts, making our first assault on clearing out the remnants of my adult life. She has been here for a week. Now enrolled at Lyndon where Link taught the last twenty years of his career, she has purchased a pre-owned yellow VW Bug for transportation to and from classes, which start next week. I have started cooking again, comfort food, mostly, since we both seem to need it. Chicken and dumplings, meatloaf, pastie, bread pudding.

We have decided on a triage formula: 1) keep; 2) pitch; 3) donate/recycle; 4) sell.

Phoebe holds up a worn pair of hand knit argyle socks. "Can I have them?" she asks. "They're really cool."

I smile. Getting rid of things is going to be harder than I feared. "I made those for your Grandpa when we were first going together. That was something girls did back then, make argyle socks for our boyfriends. Or beer mug socks with angora for the foam. I don't suppose today's girls even know how to knit."

"Knitting's kind of coming back in style, but I wouldn't make anything for a guy. By the time you've finished something, they're history." A hurt look passes across her face, a cloud over the sunrise she has been. Mentally I kick Sean Barbour in the backside for hurting her and then bless him for realizing he wasn't fit to lick her boots.

I quickly suggest, "If you're interested, I'll take you to my favorite yarn shop and we'll get us both started on something for ourselves, or each other. Not socks. They're fun because they're intricate, but probably more work than they're worth."

"Scarves are in right now," she says, smiling wanly. "And winter is coming. Snow. Cross-country skiing." Her smile improves.

The girl's got spunk. I give her a quick hug.

She opens the drawer of an old dresser in the corner of the attic, mine from when I was a child. Too "uncool" for either of my children to use, even after I antiqued it. I've dragged it around forever, using it for storage. She pulls a notebook out of the top drawer. Liesl Goehner's. I hadn't thought about it in years. "What's this?" She sits down on a box and begins paging through it. "It's all in German. Where did you get this? Oh, look, here's an envelope. Munich?"

"Grandpa and I went there once when he had to give a paper." We tried to find Mrs. Goehner's relative, the person who wrote the letter.

I remember the last time I saw Mrs. Goehner. I am surprised by the intensity of the pang I feel, for those days when I was a child, when dear Steve was a baby—-I can't believe he's sixty-six--when Carl's mother helped me get through those difficult days in the summer of 1941. Even now I would so love to know what happened to her and Mr. Goehner. To Carl. We hit a dead end in Munich. How I hope things turned out well for them all.

"Sauerbraten," she exclaims, her brown eyes alight. "I love that stuff. Let's make some, with all the trimmings. Red cabbage, potato pancakes. Black Forest cake. Good beer."

"Yes, let's." Then I think *"enemy food." That's what that old bat, Mrs. Bienenmald, called the sauerkraut I served my family during the war. What was that other expression she used? Liberty cabbage. Shades of Freedom Fries. There are fools in every generation.*

"But let's at least fill one box for Habitat first, so I don't have to feel guilty."

Phoebe has heard this before. "You were raised on guilt, right?"

"We all were. I even felt guilty that I was unable to instill guilt in my own children." We both laugh.

I reach into the back of the drawer for that old ring I had wrapped in a sock. I won it at the *Penny Arcade*, he told me. I had it appraised once, just for curiosity's sake, claiming it as a family heirloom. The ring was a good one, but not embarrassingly valuable, except for its provenance, Liesl Goehner's mother. Carl's Oma. I can't even get the ring past the first knuckle of my pinky finger.

Phoebe takes my hand and looks at the ring, then at me with a question on her face. "I bet a story goes with this."

"My first engagement ring." I shake my head. "He was nine, I was eight and a half. It was the summer your great Uncle Steve was born, the summer before Pearl Harbor."

The summer the Goehners disappeared.

Phoebe pats the old rocker, the one my mother sat on for the duration of the war. "Sit. Tell me about it, Gran. Was it romantic? Why do you still have it? Didn't he want it back? Was he cute?"

I lower myself to the chair and look at the ring. "Oh, Phoebe, that was so long ago and it's such a tangled, sad story."

"But you still remember the beginning part, don't you?" She's not going to give up, this wonderful granddaughter of mine.

"As if it were yesterday."

"And the boy who gave you the ring?"

"Carl was part of my life as far back as I can recall. And then one day he wasn't."

Face pressed against her fists, she says, "Tell me."

The story feels as if it were part of a book I started a long time ago and never finished. As if it happened to someone else.

6

Claire. The war years.
June, 1941

Chapter 3

Claire Walters looked up from her bowl of soggy corn flakes. If she didn't finish her breakfast, Mom wouldn't let her go out to play and for once, it wasn't raining. She wouldn't have to stay inside and keep Richard quiet so Mom's nerves wouldn't get on edge. With hardly any sugar, the corn flakes tasted the way she imagined hay would. Mom had skimmed the cream from the top of the bottle for her coffee, so the milk was all blue. Claire stirred her cereal and wished she had a dog to feed it to.

Her mother stood in front of the sink, rubbing her huge tummy through the shiny, striped pink top, the color of old roses. The morning sun shone through the blue checked curtains, surrounding Mom in gold light, like one of those scary religious pictures in Petey Merino's house. The Merinos were Catholics, whatever that was. Something everybody said in a whisper, so probably bad, like "adopted," or dangerous, like "radar."

"For pity's sake, Claire, finish your cereal." Already Mom sounded tired even though it was just morning. With a war on overseas and probably coming to America, Dad worked every day, even Sunday. He and three other engineers took turns driving to Sandy Hook where they worked on mysterious things they couldn't talk about except in low voices in case spies were listening.

With Daddy working every day Mom had to do everything around the house even though her baby was due any time. Claire had been warned not to mention the layette Mom had sewed or the ruffled bassinet in front of the neighbors, but she longed to tell someone. She hoped the baby would be a girl. One spoiled brother was enough. "Richard didn't finish his," she said. "Boys get away with everything."

"Please, Claire, just do as I say. For once." Mom sounded close to tears. "Think of the poor, starving...."

"I know." Claire would gladly have given her soggy corn flakes to some poor starving child in Europe. She wasn't sure exactly what Europe was, but she kind of knew *where* it was. Once, when Daddy had a rare day off, they'd driven to the shore and played in the waves. Dad had explained that Europe was on the other side of the ocean, far, far away, but not so far that the Nazis couldn't come in their boats and airplanes if America joined the Allies, whatever they were. "Okay, but, Mom, could I please have a little more sugar?"

Mom turned slowly toward her. She shrugged, then smiled sadly. "Honey, that was the last spoonful. How about some Karo? I have dark and light."

Claire nodded eagerly. "Dark." Karo wasn't very sweet, but it was fun to watch it flow slowly out of the bottle onto the cereal, making curvy swirls of brown syrup on the limp corn flakes. Karo felt nice on your tongue, too, thick and cool, like honey. Quickly she finished her cereal, pretending she was a poor starving child in Europe, dressed in rags, glad for anything at all to eat, even if it tasted like hay. "Now can I go out?"

"As long as you stay within shouting distance. I can't come running after you. What would the neighbors think?"

Why should we care what the neighbors think, Claire thought. *They don't pay our bills.* "I'm just going out in the yard." She put her bowl and spoon in the sink. At age eight she was smaller than most of her friends, not quite tall enough to see out the kitchen window, but she knew the mulberry tree in the back yard was full of berries and they would be sweet. She would pick some later.

Before going outside, she ran upstairs to her room to get her favorite book, "Cinderella." The best part was the place where Cinderella's fairy godmother touched her with a magic wand and her rags turned into a ball gown the color of sunshine. If only fairy godmothers were real. They could make all the sugar you would ever want and keep America out of the war. Then maybe Daddy wouldn't have to work every day.

Claire pushed open the screen door and let it bang shut. She loved the sharp clack of the door hitting the doorframe. For once Mom didn't yell at her to stop slamming the door. She walked down the steps and sat on the next to the bottom step, careful to pull down her skirt and keep her knees together, like a young lady. She held her book on her lap, looking around first to see if there was anything interesting happening on their street. Next door, Mrs. Bienenmald, her hair tied up in a rag like Aunt Jemima on the pancake box, was slapping rugs draped over the clothesline with a wire rug beater as if the rugs were Hitler himself. Billows of yellow dust rose into the air.

Across the street Mrs. Browne hoed the garden she'd planted between her house and the Goehner's. Claire spied Carl Goehner looking out his bedroom window on the second floor. He waved to her. She waved back, but pointed to her book. She and Carl had been friends for as long as she could remember. He understood how much she liked to read. He'd wait to come over.

A little later, just as Cinderella started to dance with Prince Charming, Claire heard the clop clop of Mr. Nishida's horse, dragging the vegetable and fruit wagon Mr. Nishida filled from his garden. Claire jumped up. "Mom, Mr. Nishida's here."

Claire's mother lumbered to the front door, wobbling from side to side like a circus bear. She handed Claire some coins and a colander. "You go," she muttered. "I don't want the neighbors to see me. See if he has a couple of nice tomatoes and some green beans. Make sure there's no bad spots."

Claire skipped down the walk, past the sidewalk, to stand next to Momoko, Mr. Nishida's horse. She reached up to pet Momoko's velvety nose. Momoko looked funny in a straw hat with holes cut out for her ears and a long black and white feather stuck in the band. Mr. Nishida looked funny in a hat that looked like an upside down straw pie tin.

"Good morning, Mrs. Walters," Mr. Nishida said, touching his forefinger to Claire's nose.

"I'm not Mrs. Walters," she protested. "That's my mother. I'm just Claire."

"But you look like a miniature Mrs. Walters, pretty like your mother," he said, smiling. Claire loved the way his eyes looked when he smiled, crinkly and sort of slanted.

I'm not pretty at all, Claire thought, but even if she wasn't, it was nice to hear.

Claire gave Momoko one last pat then walked around to look in the cart. How she longed for a peach, but Mom always said money didn't grow on trees and with the baby coming, they'd have to be more careful than ever. She picked up a tomato. On the bottom was a black spot where something had chewed on it. She put that one down. Finally she had three large perfect tomatoes that smelled wonderful. Maybe they'd have bacon and tomato sandwiches for supper. Then she selected handfuls of beans and placed them in the colander. "These beans look very fresh," she said, thinking she sounded grown up.

"I picked them this morning. The dew was still on them."

"I wish I could come see your garden and help you pick things," she said.

"If your mother lets you, I would like that very much."

Asking personal questions was rude, but Claire had wondered for a long time about Mr. Nishida's name. She didn't dare ask him what it meant, but she thought it would be all right to ask about the horse. "Why do you call her Momoko?"

He looked fondly at the little gray mare. "It means Little Peach. When I first bought her, she started eating peaches off my tree. My father, who came from Japan with my mother a long time ago and still only spoke Japanese, thought that was very funny. He gave her the name. The tree has grown quite a bit since then, but she still can reach the ones on the bottom." He patted the horse's rump. "We share, she and I."

"I love peaches, too, but with the baby...." Claire's face flamed with shame at her blunder. Please, don't let Mom have heard me, she prayed. "We have to be careful with money, in case the war comes here."

"It's a bad time all over the world," he said, shaking his head. "War is terrible. We never learn to get along, do we?"

She didn't know what to say to that, so she simply handed him the coins. "Is that enough money?"

"Maybe a little too much." He gave her ten cents back and handed her a peach. "This is from Momoko to you."

Claire pressed the peach to her nose. "It smells beautiful. Thank you, Momoko. Bye, Mr. Nishida." She placed the peach carefully on top of the string beans and started toward the house. She stopped at the steps and turned to watch the man drive his horse and cart to the corner and turn right, toward her friend Grace's house.

"That's a nice peach. Too bad you didn't get two." Carl stared at the peach hungrily. He was skinny as a squirrel even though his mom was always making fried dumplings and delicious cakes called strudel.

Claire had not seen Carl cross the street. "It's a present for me. From Momoko, Mr. Nishida's horse."

"He's a Jap," Carl said, looking in the direction Mr. Nishida had gone. "They eat dogs."

"He was born in New Jersey, Carl, so he's an American just like you," Claire said hotly. "And he doesn't eat dogs. He eats only fish and vegetables, and a little rice. He told me once. So take it back. How would you like it if people called you names?"

Carl looked away. "People do call me names."

"See?" Claire had heard them, too.

"Okay. Sorry." Carl shoved his hands in his pockets, toeing the dirt next to the walk. "You want to play?"

Poor Carl. Lately, with all the talk of war, some of the kids weren't allowed to play with him. His parents were naturalized Americans, originally from Germany. Mrs. Bienenmald had told Claire the Goehners were krauts, whatever that was, and probably Nazis, so she shouldn't get too friendly. But Claire liked the Goeh-

11

ners and Carl Goehner was her second best friend, next to Grace Peck, and besides, Grace was in Michigan for the summer.

"I have to take this in to my mother first."

"I'll wait here."

Claire thought about taking the peach with her to share with Carl, but she handed it to her mother. "It's a present. Maybe you could make something for dessert."

Claire's mother took the peach, looking as if she would cry. "You shouldn't accept presents from him."

"It wasn't exactly from him. It's from his horse. Did you know her name is...." Mom might be upset about the Japanese name. Everything seemed to upset her lately. "Her name is Little Peach because she loves peaches and she wanted me to have one because I always pet her nose and tell her how pretty she is."

"Claire Irene Walters, horses don't give presents. What an over-active imagination you have." Mom's tone was sharp, but when she put her arms around Claire, Claire knew she wasn't really mad. "I worry about you, young lady, I really do. Life isn't a fairy tale." Claire felt something poke through Mom's tummy, but when she asked if it was the baby, Mom pushed her away. "I hope your father gets home early for once."

Claire hoped so, too. Maybe Dad would feel like playing Parchesi after supper. "Can I go back outside now?"

"Yes. I'm just going to lie down for a few minutes. Please don't go far away in case I need you."

"I won't."

Mom heaved a sigh and pressed her hand against her belly.

"Does it hurt?" Claire asked.

"Of course not," Mom snapped. "This doesn't concern you."

"Sorry." Claire hung her head. Lately she didn't seem to do or say anything right.

"And check on your brother. He's down at the Merino's. I wish he'd find somebody else to play with."

"I will."

Carl was waiting on the sidewalk, kicking pebbles into the street.

When he saw her, he turned and started toward his house. "Come on. Hurry."

"Just a minute." Claire looked down the street. Richard and Petey Merino were crouching on the sidewalk, poking something with a stick. Knowing Petey, it was probably some kind of bug. Petey loved stirring up ants' nests and stamping on the ants when they ran out. Mommy didn't really like Richard playing with Petey, but Claire supposed for a little while it was all right. Hurrying to follow Carl, she called out, "Slow down. We have all day."

"I want to show you something."

"What?"

"You'll see." He ran up his driveway and ducked to scoot under the vines growing on a trellis where they always played. Claire bent down to follow. The air was cool there and smelled sweet. Pale green grapes were forming. By the end of the summer, they would be fat and purple, sweet and full of juice.

"Sit here," Carl commanded, pointing to a board covered with an old pink towel laid at the far end of the arbor. "Close your eyes and hold out your hand."

Claire squinched her eyes shut. "It's not a worm, is it? Cross your heart and hope to die?" Once Richard had dropped a worm on her hair and she'd thrown up.

"It's something nice, I promise."

Carl took her hand, pressed something cold and hard into her palm, and closed her fingers around it.

"Can I open them now?"

"Sure."

In her hand was a ring with a large green stone surrounded with tiny pearls. "Is it real?"

He shrugged as if it were nothing. "I won it at the Penny Arcade."

She looked up at him. "Are you sure you didn't steal it? It looks real."

"It's a present. Don't you like it?"

The ring looked like something her grandmother would wear, but

Carl looked so eager she didn't want to hurt his feelings. "It's very pretty."

"Put it on. It means we're engaged."

"Engaged?" She held out the ring to him. "Carl, I don't even know how to cook."

"That's okay. My mom can cook. We can live with her."

"Claire. Claire. Please come home immediately." Mom sounded funny, like she was upset about something.

Claire got up. "I have to go, Carl. Mom needs me." She tried to hand him back the ring.

"You keep it. Please. We won't get really engaged until you know how to cook and I can get a job." Carl bowed his head and stuck his hands in his pockets. "If you change your mind, you can give it back then. Okay?" He frowned and looked over his shoulder as if he thought somebody was coming. "Please?"

What was wrong with him? "Well, okay, I guess. See you." Claire hurried out from the grape arbor and headed across the street. "I'm coming, Mom. I'll be right there."

Mom was seated in her rocking chair, reading a letter written on onionskin airmail paper, her fingers splayed over her eyes as if she could not bear to look. The letter must be from Mom's cousin in England. "Claire," she cried, and grabbed onto her. "That wicked horrible man. The Germans have declared war on France and England. What will become of Violet and her children? Her husband has gone and joined up to fight." She held Claire so tight Claire could scarcely breathe.

If Mom was scared, would something bad happen to them, too? Was there anything she could do to help?

* * *

The baby came that night, not a girl, but another boy. Children weren't allowed in hospitals unless they were sick, so Claire and Richard waited in the parking lot, locked in the car, while Dad went in to see the new baby. He would be called Stephen.

The night was inky black when Claire heard Dad unlock the car door. Dad looked in the back where she and Richard waited,

14

wrapped in quilts. "Everything's fine," he told them in a voice that was both happy and tired.

"It's a boy, huh, Daddy?" Richard asked in a proud voice.

"Yup, and he's a fine specimen."

"Ha ha, Claire," Richard said. "Told you."

"You baby," she whispered. "When can I see Mom?"

"In a few days, when she and Stephen come home. Mrs. Bienenmald will take care of you two while I'm at work." Dad started the engine and headed for home.

Claire wanted to protest. She didn't like Mrs. Bienenmald one bit, but Daddy probably didn't have anybody else to ask. Mom would be home soon and everything would be fine.

She looked out the window at the telephone lines and treetops. The sky was cloudy again. Probably it would rain in the morning. She felt the ring in her dress pocket. Maybe tomorrow, if she asked really nicely, Mrs. Bienenmald would let Carl play at her house. Or, better yet, let her go over to Carl's house.

Just a few more days.

Chapter
4

When Daddy woke Claire up the next morning, rain was falling, making soft whispery sounds on the leaves of the maple tree outside her window. "Come on, honey. Time to get up."

Getting up was the last thing Claire wanted to do. "Feels like we just went to bed," she grumbled, rubbing her eyes.

"I'm sorry, Bug. I know it was late, but I have to get ready for work. Gotta pack my own lunch today. The guys'll really laugh when they see what I bring." He chuckled, but he sounded cross.

"I could do that for you, Daddy. I know how to make two kinds of sandwiches. Tuna fish and peanut butter and jelly. I could wrap them in wax paper and put them in your lunch box with some cookies and a thermos of milk, just like Mom does. You can have my peach, too." She didn't mention that Momoko had given it to her. Daddy would think she was crazy.

He gave her a quick hug. "I know you could, but I'll manage for today and your mother will be back in no time. Mrs. Bienenmald will feed you while I'm at work. You can take a nap there if you want."

Claire dressed in what she'd worn the day before. Daddy grabbed some clothes for Richard and carried his son fireman style next door, splashing through the puddles that filled the bare spots in the lawn. Claire followed daddy and tried to watch where she was going, but the clouds made it gloomy and hard to see. She stepped in one of the puddles and got her feet wet. She was glad she'd carried her shoes and socks, or she's have been in trouble since it was her only pair. She wiped her feet carefully on the rag rug outside the kitchen door. Mrs. Bienenmald would shriek like a banshee, whatever that was, if anyone made wet tracks on her linoleum.

Mrs. Bienenmald, in a baggy print dress and flowered apron, shuffled from the sink to the stove, pausing to flip the buckwheat pancakes and turn the single strip of bacon apiece she'd planned for Claire and Richard's breakfast. She served the pancakes with Karo, the dark kind. Claire hated the taste of buckwheat, but supper the night before had been peanut butter and bread eaten standing in the kitchen, while Daddy carried Mom's suitcase out to the car, so she was hungry. She ate the pancakes quickly, pretending she was the winning contestant in a pancake-eating contest. She washed the taste away with milk.

Richard, in rumpled blue pajamas, sat at the table trying manfully to eat, but his eyes kept closing, opening, then closing again, until he fell back to sleep in his chair with his mouth open.

"Poor baby," Mrs. Bienenmald crooned. "I'll save these for later." She set Richard's plate on the counter and then picked him up with a grunt. "Your father said you didn't get much sleep last night."

"No, we didn't." Claire wondered if it was all right to mention the baby, now that he was born and had a name. Better not. Maybe Mom was planning to say she found Stephen in the cabbage patch.

She followed Mrs. Bienenmald into the living room and watched her lay Richard on the sofa and cover him with an afghan made of crocheted squares in orange and pink.

"Can Carl come over to play today, Mrs. Bienenmald? It's too rainy to play outside." She stuck her hand in the dress pocket to feel for the ring and remembered she'd put it in her sock drawer when they got home from the hospital the night before.

Mrs. Bienenmald turned around with a scowl on her face. "What a selfish girl you are, Claire. How do you expect your poor little brother to sleep with you and that boy making a racket?"

"We wouldn't make a racket," Claire said, miffed. "We'd just play Monopoly, or checkers, on the porch."

"You think you wouldn't make a racket, but I know you, young lady." She started for the kitchen, hands clenched, slippers flapping. "With all the nice children there are in this neighborhood, why you have to play with that kraut boy is beyond me."

Claire followed her trying to make her understand. "Carl's American and he's my friend. Besides, the other kids won't play with him, and that's *not* nice."

"Well, I should think they wouldn't." Mrs. Bienenmald raised Claire's plate and set it in the dishpan. "Those Gohners are just trouble."

"It's pronounced Gayner," Claire said.

Mrs. Bienenmald sighed. "When people live in America, they should pronounce their name like Americans, unless they want people to think they're spies."

"Spies? Walters is an English name. My great grandpa came from England." She sat back in her chair, swinging her feet.

"For pity's sake, sit still, young lady."

Claire crossed her legs at the ankles. "What kind of name is Bienenmald?" Claire flinched when she saw Mrs. Bienenmald's open hand. Mrs. Bienenmald didn't slap her, but she looked ready to.

"It's American and don't you forget it." She cleaned the table with a savage swipe of a dishcloth. "If you love them so much, you can go over there, but don't come crying to me when those Nazis get in trouble."

Why would they get in trouble? Who with? "They're not Nazis." Whatever they were.

"You're a child. What do you know?"

I know a lot. Claire got out of her chair and pushed it in. She would not give Mrs. Bienenmald anything to criticize. "Thank you for breakfast. It was delicious. And thank you for letting me play with Carl."

Claire heard her mutter "They probably keep a picture of Hitler in their house," but she kept on walking toward the front door. She closed the screen door carefully so it wouldn't slam and started across the street. She had a question for Mrs. Goehner.

* * *

Carl's mother was chopping vegetables at the kitchen table.

Claire knocked on the back door. "Hi, Mrs. Goehner. Can Carl play?"

Carl's mother looked up from her work and smiled. "Claire. Come in. Carl is now upstairs getting dressed. How are you today?"

Claire sighed. "I'm kind of tired."

"So, the baby was born last night? Is it a boy or a girl?"

Claire's eyes went wide. "How did you know?"

Mrs. Goehner laughed, but her eyes were red. "Well, once you have a child of your own, you know when someone else is expecting. Did you think it was a secret, then?"

Claire nodded. "I'm not supposed to tell."

Liesl Goehner reached to pat Claire's cheek. "You didn't. But I have eyes." She motioned toward a chair. "Sit, then. I have some ginger cake with raisins just warm from the oven. Would you like?"

"Yes, please. Mrs. Bienenmald made buckwheat pancakes." She couldn't suppress a shudder.

Liesl laughed. "I don't like them either. This the bad taste will take away." She got up and cut a piece of cake and poured a small glass of milk. The glass was one of those that came with cheese spread inside and had red stars all over it. Claire loved those glasses. And she loved Mrs. Goehner.

"The baby is a boy but I was hoping for a baby sister." She sighed. "His name is Stephen."

Mrs. Goehner laughed. "We need boys, too, but I understand you are disappointed. A sister is a good thing to have. Mine is far away. I worry about her, with that war, that terrible man." She wiped her hands on her apron and went outside.

Claire stood up and went to the window to see what Carl's mother was doing. Mrs. Goehner headed straight for the garden. She picked up some kind of garden tool and dug in the dirt, pull-

19

ing out a large onion. She brushed off the clumps of dirt and held the onion to her nose, then in front of her admiring it as if it were a jewel. A look of sadness passed over her face. After a moment she came inside, washed the onion, and chopped it into small pieces on a wooden cutting board. Carefully she scraped every piece into the pot on the stove and then dabbed at her eyes with her apron.

"Why are you crying, Mrs. Goehner?"

"Ach, no. I do not cry. It is just the onion."

She was crying Claire saw, but often it seemed to her grownups didn't tell the truth, even though they expected kids to. What was wrong about crying? Also she wanted to be sure the Goehners were not Nazis, but that was probably not something she should ask.

Claire pressed her nose against the cake to smell the ginger and cinnamon before eating it. She took little bites, followed by tiny sips of milk, to make the deliciousness last.

Finally Carl came clomping downstairs. When he saw his mother he ran and put his arms around her. "Don't cry, Mama. Everything will be fine."

"I do not cry," she insisted, hugging him. "It is the onion. Your friend is here."

He nodded at Claire and pulled away from his mother. "Hi, Claire. I saw you cross the street. All it ever does around here is rain, rain, rain." He walked over to sniff the ginger cake. "Is this for breakfast?"

"Toast and eggs first."

After breakfast, Carl got out his checkerboard. Claire and he sat on the back porch and played until noon when Carl's mother called. "Richard is here, Claire. You must go back for lunch"

Claire helped put the game back in the box, then walked through the kitchen. She saw what Mrs. Goehner had prepared for lunch "What's that? It smells good."

"Split peas cooked with onions and broth. You just follow the directions on the bag. The onions will make you cry. Then you cut up frankfurters and arrange like so, so it looks nice. Serve with

20

some nice bread and butter, and you won't go hungry."

Claire was sure it was better than what she'd have across the street. "I wish I could cook."

Car laughed so hard he almost choked.

"Carl, what is wrong with you?" his mother asked, but he only laughed harder and Claire blushed.

"Silly boy. Now, Claire, remember this. If you can read, you can cook." Mrs. Goehner put her hands on Claire's cheeks. "Just don't be in a hurry. Good food takes time. I am glad the Depression is over. Once in the old country my cousins had only grass and wild onions to make soup."

Aghast, Claire blurted, "That must have tasted terrible."

Carl's mother laughed in her sad way. "They said it tasted like hay, but it filled their bellies. Now we have plenty but over there, they still have not much to eat, even less with the war on."

"Come on, Claire," Richard whined. "Mrs. Beanbag's getting mad."

"What's for lunch?"

"Tuna fish with sweet relish." Richard clutched his stomach and pretended to throw up.

"When you are grown," Mrs. Goehner said, "you can fix your food how you like it."

"I'll never be grown up." Richard turned away, head down, hands clenched.

Mrs. Goehner laughed softly. "Grown up comes too soon." She gave Claire a quick hug. "You're a good girl, Claire. Remember that always."

Claire hugged her back. "Thanks for the cake and milk. It was delicious and it did take the bad taste away."

Mrs. Goehner laughed. "Any time, Claire, you are welcome."

"Hurry" Richard urged.

With a sense of dread, Claire followed Richard back across the street.

Chapter
5

Claire heard the robins before she even opened her eyes. Their morning song, sweetly announcing the sun, was her favorite of all the birds' calls. She smiled. Mom and Baby Stephen were coming home this morning, after five long days in the hospital. She could hardly wait.

The day before, she and Dad had bought food, cleaned the house, and done the wash. How proud she had been when she had to show Dad how to push the wet clothes through the wringer. Even the weather had cooperated by not raining. They had pinned the sheets on the line to dry in sunshine instead of down in the basement where things never really smelled quite right afterward. Even Richard had helped for once, folding towels and putting underwear and socks in piles on the dining room table.

Having Mom back meant Claire would have more time to read and play with Carl. He seemed so worried lately and when she asked, he just shook his head and said he was fine.

Claire stretched and smiled again. She slipped out from under the sheet and put her feet on the cool, bare floor. Before Dad got up she'd check to make sure they hadn't missed anything. She tiptoed downstairs and walked through the living room. She could still see the paths she had made on the gray carpet with the new Electrolux. Mom's Woman's Days and Better Homes and Gardens were neatly arranged on the coffee table, pillows set just so on the couch. Her maroon chenille knitting bag with the unfinished baby sweater, yellow because you never knew what the baby would be, was on the floor, tucked next to the rocker.

Flowers! Claire ran to get scissors from the kitchen and skipped outside. The grass, cool and dewy in the early morning, felt lovely on her bare feet. She snipped several yellow climbing roses that smelled just like honey, a handful of blue bachelor's buttons, and a couple of pinks. After wiping bits of wet grass from her feet on the rag rug outside the kitchen door, she went inside and found the glass pitcher Mom always used for flowers. She filled it half full of water and wiped the sides so it wouldn't be slippery before carrying the flowers upstairs to put on Mom's bedside table. Dad had warned that Mom might still have to spend a few more days in bed. Having a baby, he'd explained in a sad voice, was hard on a woman.

Having a baby was hard on everybody, Claire decided.

Daddy was still asleep, lying on his stomach, his face turned toward where Claire was carefully placing the flowers. As she set down the vase, his eyes opened. He grunted. The skin around his eyes crinkled. He was smiling.

"These are for Mom."

Dad pushed up and turned over, scratching his chest through the opening in his pajama top. He leaned toward the vase, sniffed, and nodded. "She'll love those, Bug, especially the roses."

"The bachelor's buttons are for me," Claire admitted.

"I know. Same blue as your eyes." Dad got out of bed, paused to pinch Claire's nose between his fore and middle fingers, and headed out to the hall and down to the bathroom. "Could you get your brother up and maybe start breakfast? Cereal's fine."

Richard, still in bed but already awake and playing with his red and blue celluloid boat, was talking to himself. No, Claire realized, he was talking to Joe Clark Bar. Named for the candy Dad sometimes brought home for a treat, Joe had been Richard's imaginary friend for more than a year. "After breakfast, let's take the sailboat over to Mrs. Bienenmald's fish pond, Joe. The old meany won't even know we're there."

"Time to get up." Claire tugged at the sheet. "Come on, Richard. We have to go get Mom."

"Don't you think I know it?" Richard said, glaring at her. "I'm not a baby." He pushed the covers back and stood up on the bed, making a few tentative bounces, watching his sister from behind lowered eyelids. Jumping on the bed was not allowed.

"Good thing," Claire said. "We have a new baby and you're going to have to help."

"That's girl's work," Richard said with a sneer.

We'll see about that, Claire vowed to herself. "Get dressed. No jumping." She tossed the striped shirt and short pants they'd put out the night before at his feet. "Don't forget clean underwear."

Richard pulled at the front of his pajama bottom. "I have to go. Number One. Really bad."

"Dad's in the bathroom. You'll just have to wait."

"No, I can't." Richard jumped off the bed and ran downstairs making airplane noises. In a moment he was out in the back yard, squeezing in between the leafy branches of the lilac bush where he and Joe played "bus."

Claire stood in the kitchen doorway and watched as a steaming yellow stream shot out from the lilac leaves, all she could see of her brother. She shook her head and turned away. Boys! And now they had another one.

She went back inside and got out the blue and white cereal bowls and glasses for juice. She gave Richard the chipped glass with blue stars and kept the red tulip one for herself. She got out the bottle of milk and shook it to mix in the cream. They could have Wheaties or Rice Krispies. Dad would have to make his own coffee; she was afraid of the percolator. She put out spoons and paper napkins, folding them neatly in half, the way Mom did.

She realized she hadn't dressed either and ran upstairs to put on her blue dress and new sandals and to smooth out her bed, easy to do since it was too hot this time of year for anything but a sheet.

As she passed the bathroom she could smell Dad's spicy shaving cream and hear him whistling "In A Persian Market," his shaving song. Daddy was funny. She loved him so much.

She skipped down the stairs, thinking ahead to when Mom would be home and everything would go back to the way it was supposed to be.

* * *

The first thing she noticed when the nurse wheeled Mom to the car was how pale Mom was, and how tired she looked. She hadn't even combed her hair very well. Dad helped Mom into the front seat and turned to Claire with a pleading look. "Do you think you can hold the baby? Mom's still a little shaky."

Claire took a good look at her mother. Why didn't she even say hello? Maybe when they got home and Mom saw how nice Claire and Dad had made everything, she would feel happier.

"Sure, Daddy." Claire sat up straighter and shot a look of triumph at her brother, proud to be treated like a grownup, but Richard was looking out the window, pointing out the ambulance to Joe. Dad had insisted Joe stay home the night Stephen was born, but gave in when Richard begged to bring his friend to pick up the baby.

Claire cradled the small warm bundle all wrapped in a pale green blanket. She could smell his breath, so sweet, and the baby powder. Poor Stephen wasn't very cute. His face was red, his skin spotty, and he had a very big mouth. In his favor he had lots of dark hair and little fingers with nails that reminded Claire of the tiny gold shells she liked to gather at the bay.

As they drove away, Stephen's eyes opened. He looked frightened. His lower lip quivered and he made a soft bleat. Claire held him closer and patted his tiny back. "It's okay, Stephen. We're going home and it's a really beautiful day."

As soon as she stopped talking, he whimpered, so she started up again. "Your new bed's all ready for you with a brand new sheet with bears on it and a blanket Nana crocheted for you. Your bed's called a bassinet. I don't know why. Your clothes are a layette, whatever that is, and we'll give you a bath in the Bathinet. That sounds like baby talk, doesn't it? We don't like baby talk, do we? We'll just call it a tub. What do you say about that, even if it doesn't rhyme?"

She later insisted that Stephen had smiled at her little joke, but everyone said it was just gas.

Chapter
6

Claire got up with the sun and stole downstairs to pack Daddy's lunch. She tore off two pieces of wax paper and laid them on the kitchen table. From the wrapped loaf of white bread in the breadbox she took four thick slices. Carefully she spread each piece with mayonnaise and laid two rounds of bologna and one slice of yellow American cheese on two of the bread slices. She added some of Mrs. Goehner's garden lettuce and wrapped the sandwiches after cutting them into diagonal sections. She opened Daddy's black metal lunch box and set the sandwiches, a handful of gingersnaps, and a plum inside. She washed out the thermos with warm soapy water, rinsed with cold, and then filled it with milk.

By the time her father came downstairs, she had made toast and scrambled eggs that were only a little overcooked. Dad sat at the table and drank his juice in one gulp, as if it were medicine. "This looks great, Bug. You're getting to be as good a cook as your grandmother." His smile didn't look quite real, but Claire could tell he was trying his best. He picked up his fork and, with a quick glance at the kitchen clock, dug in. "I think your mother's a little better today."

Mom had been home for two weeks and she still had only gotten out of bed to take a bath a couple of times. "She's awake?"

"Yes. I think so." He rubbed his eyes and let out a small sigh. "She was, for a minute."

"I'll take her some breakfast later." Claire wished she dared make coffee. Mom would like that. Probably.

Out front a car horn honked. Shave and a haircut. Two bits!

26

Dad swallowed the last bit of egg and stood up. He grabbed his lunchbox and the second piece of toast. "Tell you what, tonight I'll fill the coffeepot after supper. I know you don't want to do that, but you could turn it on in the morning. You're not afraid to do that, are you? You just fixed eggs."

"I'm not afraid, not anymore, and Mom'll like it," Claire said, thinking she'd try to pour off some of the top milk into a jar for Mom's coffee. "Don't worry, Dad. I'll take care of everything."

"That's my girl."

After he rushed out the back door, Claire realized she had called him "Dad" instead of "Daddy." She wondered if he'd noticed. Well, she was past the age of calling him "Daddy."

She rinsed the dishes and put them in the dishpan. She'd wash them after Richard ate his cereal. She opened the toaster flaps and put in two slices of bread.

From upstairs came an earsplitting howl. Stephen. After unplugging the toaster, Claire went upstairs. "I'm coming, you little bunny rabbit." Stephen stopped crying the moment she entered the room. She tossed a diaper over her shoulder and lifted him. "Oh, you little stinky boy. It's okay. I'll change you." She held him a moment to savor his sweet baby warmth before laying him on the bathinet.

She pulled off the rubber pants and unpinned the diaper. At least he was only wet, but his poor little bottom was fiery red. When she wiped him with a damp washcloth, he let out a hair-raising scream.

"Claire! What in heaven's name are you doing to that baby?"

"Just changing him, Mom. He's all chapped."

"Well, for heaven's sake, Claire. Shame on you."

Claire fought against the rush of anger. Mom was sick, Stephen's bottom was red as a beet, and she was doing her best.

The baby oil seemed to soothe him, and soon they were downstairs. Claire sat in the rocking chair in the living room and held him while he greedily sucked down his formula, making little baby grunts of satisfaction. A rush of love swept through Claire. She

27

would do anything for this baby. Her baby. For now.

* * *

"Mom?" Claire tiptoed into the darkened room carrying a plate. Only a slight rustle of sheet told Claire her mother was awake. "Mom?"

"What is it, Claire?" her mother asked between clenched teeth.

"I made you some toast, with strawberry jam. Tomorrow Dad and I will make coffee."

"Can't you see I'm sleeping?" Mom sounded like she was crying. "For heaven's sake, Claire. What's the matter with you?"

Claire blinked to hide the sudden surge of tears. "I'm sorry, Mom. I thought you'd like some breakfast."

"Just keep that baby quiet. Is that too much to ask?"

"I'll do my best. Sorry."

Mom snuffled. "I'm sorry, too, Claire. I don't know what's wrong with me. I'm just so tired."

Claire took the plate of toast downstairs and set it on the table. Maybe Mom would want it later. Maybe she would eat it herself, for lunch, so it wouldn't go to waste.

Richard had left his cereal bowl on the table, but at least he'd finished most of it. Claire didn't have the heart to yell at him to come in and put it in the sink where he was supposed to. Richard wasn't looking very happy himself lately.

She went outside to find him, to offer him Mom's toast. He was slumped on the edge of the sandbox, digging a hole in the dirt with a stick. The sand had been gone for over a year. "You want some toast? It's got that strawberry jam Nana sent."

He looked up sullenly and rubbed his eyes with his fists. "Why is everybody mad at me?"

"I'm not mad at you, Richard. Dad's just busy." She sat down next to him. "And Mom's tired."

"Yeah, I know." He took a piece of toast from the plate. "You can have the other one."

Touched, she said, "Thanks," and took a bite. As she and Richard munched on their toast, they watched Mrs. Bienenmald waddle across her back yard with a wicker basket full of wash on her hip. She shot them both a dirty look, making them giggle and cover their mouths so she wouldn't yell. She pinned three pairs of giant pink underpants on the line and quickly covered them with pillowcases. "Grownups are funny," Claire said, when Mrs. Bienenmald hung Mr. Bienenmald's white undershorts for the whole world to see.

Once, long before Mom had Stephen, Mom had told Dad that Mrs. Bienenmald made her husband's undershorts out of sailcloth, whatever that was, so they'd last. Dad made the funniest face. "No wonder Jimmy B. walks so funny." He and Mom had laughed a lot. It had been a nice sound. Maybe someday soon Claire would hear them laugh again.

"I wish we had a dog," Richard said through a mouthful of toast. "I could play with him and take him for walks. I'd call him Buddy. Buddy Clark Bar."

"What if it was a girl dog?"

"A girl dog?" Richard laughed so hard he fell off the side of the sandbox. Toast crumbs sputtered from his mouth. He lay on the grass and looked up at the sky. "I'd take it to the puppy store and tell them to give me my money back. Dogs should be boys. Buddy would be Joe's little brother."

"I didn't know Joe was a dog." She reached for Richard's hand and pulled him up. "Is he?"

Richard shook his head and scowled. "Is Mommy gonna get better soon?"

"Everybody says she will."

He pressed his cheeks against his knuckles. "How come she doesn't like me anymore?"

"She loves you, Richard, but right now she has the baby blues."

"You mean because it's a boy? Is she sad because Stephen's a boy? I'm a boy."

"She would have them even if it had been a girl."

"But wouldn't she have the baby pinks then?"

Claire laughed. "You are so funny, Richard. Having the blues means that you're sad. It has nothing to do with what color the baby's clothes are."

"Oh, I get it," he said, but Claire didn't think he did.

Before she could explain further, she heard the phone ring. People didn't call very often these days. She tore into the house to answer before the ringing disturbed Mom. She held the earpiece to her ear and clutched the stand in her other hand, pretending she was talking into a daffodil. "Hello?" she said, using her grownup voice. To her ears she sounded a lot like Mom, from before.

"Claire? This is Nana. How's that new baby coming along?"

"He's fine, Nana. He's really getting cute. At first he didn't look so good, but he's starting to look like a person."

"Well, that's the idea. Is he eating?"

"Just formula. He's too little for solid food yet." That's what Aunt Barbara, Dad's sister, had told Claire. That was the kind of thing grownups said.

"What about your mother? Your dad said she was off her feed, whatever he meant by that."

Claire decided not to answer that question. "She's in bed right now. She's sleeping."

"Hasn't she been up at all?"

Claire didn't want to tell on her mother. She crossed her fingers. "Well, sometimes she does."

"Who's taking care of the baby, for pity's sake?"

"I am. Dad says I'm doing a good job, a very good job."

"I'm sure you are, for a child, but a baby needs its mother. You go tell that daughter of mine her mother is calling, long distance, and she'd better come to the telephone right this minute. This is ridiculous. She needs to get out of that bed and take care of things. She's a grown woman, with responsibilities."

"She's just tired, Nana. She has the blues. The baby blues."

"Oh, fiddle. She has a family to take care of and you have no business knowing about such things, Claire Irene. Shame on you. You're a child. Now go get her."

Claire sighed. She knew more about the blues than she wanted to. She set down the telephone, noticing how dusty the tabletop was. Dad and she hadn't cleaned since Mom came home. Taking care of a house was endless. All you ever did was work and work and do the same things over and over again and then it was time to begin once more. Maybe she could dust while Stephen was taking a nap.

"Claire? Claire?" Nana's voice sounded like Mickey Mouse coming from the receiver. "Do as I say, young lady. Do you hear me?"

Claire made a face and ran up the stairs and into her parents' bedroom. "Mom. It's Nana. She's calling long distance."

Mom lay on her back, looking at the ceiling. She closed her eyes. "Well, of course she is, Claire. She's in Ohio."

Claire wanted to scream, but she bit her lip and counted to ten. "She wants you to come to the phone."

"I'm sure she does." Mom turned on her side and pulled the sheet over her head. "Just let me alone."

Downstairs Stephen, who had been happily settled in his playpen watching the sun filter through the kitchen window, let out a wail. Claire looked at the tangle of sheets on the bed, shrugged, and ran downstairs. If Stephen made a racket, Mom might get worse.

Stephen was sprawled on his back, bellowing, his little face crumpled in rage, his feet kicking out. Claire ran to the door. "Richard, I need your help. Please come here."

He trudged in, trailing dirt on his bare feet. "What for?"

"Get the phone. Tell Nana Stephen needs to be changed and Mom is asleep. She'll just have to call back tonight when Dad's here."

Poor baby was drenched and she had forgotten his rubber pants.

Finally she got him oiled and changed again. His bottom didn't look any better. She decided to put him in his carriage and take him for a walk. If he cried, Mom wouldn't hear him and maybe Mrs. Goehner would be out. Maybe she knew what to do for rashes.

* * *

Richard held onto the carriage as they walked. "Nana said you were a bad girl for not coming back to the phone. She said you were not sponsable, or something like that. She sounded mad."

Claire hung her head and pushed the carriage harder. She was doing more than everybody else, except Dad. They headed up the block.   Petey Merino was out in his front yard, stamping on anthills. When he saw them, he stopped and came over to the carriage.

"Who's that?"

"Stephen," Claire said. She wanted to say it was none of his business.

Petey made a face. "We went to the movies last night," he said. "In the newsreel the U-boats were sinking passenger boats with tor, tor-something."

"Torpedoes?" Claire kept walking. She didn't want to hear about torpedoes and sinking ships.

He galloped after them. "Yeah. Them. The water was full of people screaming and there was blood everywhere, only it was all black and white so you couldn't tell if it was blood or just water. But my dad said it was blood." He grinned. "It was really neat. I mean, awful."

"Petey!" his mother called. "I told you to stay in the yard."

"Yeah, yeah." He slunk away.

"Is that true, Claire?"

"Don't pay any attention to him, Richard. He...he has an overactive imagination." They continued on their walk, passing the firehouse, the Lutheran church, Dr. Rosenthal's office with the red roses climbing over a white trellis, and back home. She looked across the street, hoping to see Carl at his window, or playing outside, but he was nowhere to be seen. She decided to go anyway. Mrs. Goehner wouldn't yell if she knocked on their door.

Just seeing Carl's mother kneeling in her garden, pulling weeds, a big straw hat covering her blond hair, made Claire feel better.

"Claire. And Richard. Is that the new little one?" Liesl Goehner jumped up and ran to peer into the carriage. "Oh, so dear, so little. Will your mother mind if I hold him?"

"She'll just be glad if he's not screaming so she can sleep," Claire said.

"Oh, little one," Mrs. Goehner crooned, holding him against her shoulder. "Does he scream, then?"

"Only when I change him. He has a really bad rash. I put baby oil on him, but it still looks really sore. I don't know what else to do."

Mrs. Goehner gave her a quick hug. "Let me look." She carried Stephen to the grassy part of the yard. She spread out his blanket and took off his diaper, sticking the safety pins into the front of her dress. "Oh, ja. See. Poor thing." Stephen whimpered. "Come close, Claire. He worries when you are not near. We can just leave him without his diaper. Sunshine and warm air helps clear this up."

Claire looked around. What would Mrs. Brown think if she saw a naked baby outside?

"It is nothing, Claire. He is just a boy, like all other boys. Just like Richard. Just like Carl. Nothing new."

Richard's face turned red and he looked away.

Carl's mother laughed. "Sometimes you Americans are funny about natural things, I think. Of course, my Carl is American, but he is not so silly." She pushed to her feet. "Did you children eat this morning?"

"I had a piece of toast," Claire admitted.

"I had Wheaties," Richard said, pushing back the sleeve of his polo shirt to show his muscles. "Breakfast of Champions. And toast. Claire made it."

Mrs. Goehner smiled. "So. I have been cooking this morning. I bring you some milk and peach strudel. Ja?"

"Sure," Richard exclaimed. "Strudel."

Claire and Richard drank milk and ate strudel while Stephen kicked his legs in the sunny air and made bubbles with his lips. In the garden a couple of bees buzzed through the zinnias. Somewhere a cardinal called. So peaceful here, Claire thought. Not like at home, even though it was quiet. The quiet was loud somehow.

She finished her milk and lay back on the grass, feeling happy, full, and, for no reason she could have explained, very sad. Overhead puffy clouds bumped along, brilliant white in a flag blue sky. Richard flopped down alongside her, stretching his arms and legs as if he were making snow angels.

He pointed toward one of the clouds. "That one looks like a fat clown."

"No, it doesn't. It looks like a bunny."

"You think everything looks like a bunny. It looks like a soldier," he insisted.

"A bear, maybe."

"Well, that one looks like a dirigible." Richard sat up; his eyes widened. "Maybe the Germans are coming to bomb us."

Watching Mrs. Goehner pull weeds from among the tomatoes, Claire shoved her elbow into Richard's side. "Don't say that."

"But what if they are?"

Claire had no answer and Mrs. Goehner didn't seem to have heard Richard's remark.

"Sunny days we have been having this week." Mrs. Goehner raised her face to the sky. "It would be good for your mother to come outside. Sunshine is good for more things than rashes."

"Even the baby blues?"

"Well, you would need more than sunshine, but it would help, I think." Carl's mother sat down on the grass near them with a colander of peas and began shelling them into a yellow bowl.

"Did you have the baby blues after Carl was born?" Claire blushed. "Sorry. I shouldn't have asked. Nana says I have no business knowing about such things."

Liesl Goehner clucked her tongue. "Someday you will have babies, Claire. They don't come from under cabbage plants or from a stork. You should know about those things, and, anyway, how could you not know? You are for now the housewife and your mother is very sad. Before you go, I give you something for your dinner. Your father is gone all the day working so hard. He will need good food. You can help me. Maybe your mother will eat, too."

"She wouldn't even eat the toast I made for her this morning.

Nana says she needs to snap out of it."

"Claire dear, it does not snap out, just like that." Carl's mother did not explain further, but for a moment her hand rested on Claire's shoulder. How did she know? But Claire didn't ask. There were so many things you shouldn't talk about.

Minutes later Carl and his father came back in their big brown car with packages from the hardware store. While they stowed the packages in the garage, Claire put Stephen's diaper and rubber pants back on so he wouldn't get sunburned on his bottom, which would be just as bad as a rash. Stephen yawned and stretched. His eyelids fluttered. "Time for a nap, bunny boy." Claire put him in the carriage and turned it away from the sun to shade his eyes.

"Come, Claire. The men can watch Stephen while he sleeps. I show you how to make something easy. First we get some tomatoes from the garden, and green beans. They are just ripe. You take potatoes and a bit of ham, and it's a good dinner."

* * *

Mom would only nibble on a piece of dry toast in bed. Dad ate as if he had never seen food before, smiling and telling Claire and Richard about the volley ball game they played at work during lunch hour, all the while sopping up the lovely gravy with Mrs. Goehner's homemade bread.

In the morning when Dad left for work he told Claire to be sure to thank Mrs. Goehner again for the delicious meal. "And thank you, Claire Bug, for my lunch. You are my angel." He kissed the top of her head and rushed out the door.

Claire stood on the stool Dad had made for her as she filled the dishpan. "I think," she said to the robin in the tree outside the kitchen window, "it's much too hard to be an angel. When I grow up, I'm going to be an architect. I'll have my own angel to clean for me."

At first she thought Richard was laughing, but then she realized he was shouting. "Get your gun. Run, Joe. Run. Ack ack ack ack! Got him!"

Standing on tiptoe Claire looked through the kitchen window

35

into the back yard. Richard was hiding in the lilac bush. He and Joe Clark Bar weren't playing bus today. They were shooting Germans.

Chapter
7

Today was as hot as any August day, but the night before a thread of coolness in the evening air reminded Claire that school would be starting soon. Who would take care of Stephen?

She pinned a fresh diaper on Stephen and slipped on his rubber pants. He kicked his feet and stretched, grunting softly. How sweet he was. She picked him up and kissed his cheek.

She stopped in the bathroom to drop the soiled diaper in the toilet and left it to soak. She'd put it in the diaper pail later. Right now she needed to talk to Dad. For some unknown reason Dad's boss had given him a whole Sunday off.

First thing after breakfast Dad had mowed the lawn. Now he and Richard were raking up the cut grass in piles and tossing it into a couple of old peach baskets, but not hurrying. In fact, they were leaning on their rakes, talking.

Claire carried Stephen out to where Dad and Richard stood. They looked like Mutt and Jeff from the funny papers in matching striped shirts except that Richard wore short pants and Dad wore some old work pants that had a rip in the knee. Claire wished she knew how to fix things. It hurt to see Dad wearing ragged clothes. Maybe Mrs. Goehner could teach her about sewing.

The sun sifted through the leaves of the mulberry tree, making shifting patterns of shade on the ground. Birds twittered in the bushes near Mrs. Bienenmald's pond. A yellow butterfly flitted among the climbing roses. As Claire passed into full sun, Stephen blinked and sneezed. Dad and Richard turned around, smiled at the baby, but kept talking.

"Is there going to be a war, Daddy?" Richard asked.

"Why would you think that, Bud?"

"Because it's on the radio all the time. Mrs. Browne's son got drafted to be a soldier, just like the old crab's grandson."

"Is that any way to talk, Richard?" Dad covered his mouth and rubbed his forefinger over his upper lip.

"No, but she is."

"I assume you're talking about Mrs. B. from next door?"

"Mrs. Bee? Mrs. Bumblebee?" Richard slapped himself on the forehead and fell down on the ground laughing. "Bzz, bzz, and then she stings you."

Dad shook his finger playfully at Richard. "Now you know that's not nice. I meant 'B' as in Bienenmald." He lowered himself to the ground and reached for Stephen. "I'll take him for a bit." He spread Stephen's blanket on the ground and laid him on it. He held out a forefinger and grinned when Stephen grabbed onto it.

"Carl says 'Biene' is German for 'bee.' His mother is teaching him German." Claire and Richard looked at one another and giggled. "He thinks 'mald' doesn't mean anything."

"It means 'meany,'" Richard said.

"Name calling is just the beginning," Dad said.

"So, is there, Daddy? Going to be a war?"

Dad spread his hands, palm up. "Roosevelt promised us that no American boys would be sent overseas. I hope that's true."

"I'm an American boy. If there's a war, will they send me? Will I have to fight German boys my same age?" Richard covered his face with his hands. "I don't want to miss kindergarten."

"He meant big boys, Richard, at least eighteen years old." Dad sighed. "Not that eighteen is very old."

"Do you believe Roosevelt, Dad? Really and truly, cross your heart?" Claire asked.

Dad rested his head in his hands for a long moment before turning to look at her. "I believed him when he said it, but he was running for re-election, so who knows? Hitler's already tearing up Europe. We may have to help. War is the most terrible thing mankind can do. My Uncle John was wounded in the Great War. He was never the same."

"I remember him," Claire said.

"You do?"

"Very well."

Dad smiled at her. "You never cease to amaze me, Claire Bug."

"We visited him once in some hospital on the way to Nana's when I was four and Richard was a baby."

"That's right. I'm surprised you remember that. He's lived in a veteran's hospital since 1918. He wanted to be an architect."

Like me. Claire counted on her fingers. "Twenty-three years." She remembered that Great Uncle John had sat in a wheelchair with a crocheted afghan over his lap, talking to himself, babbling mostly. He had only one arm and no idea who Dad was, but he was glad to get the chewing gum Claire gave him and said thank you over and over again. He was still saying it when they left. Her heart hurt just thinking about him.

"What if they make you be a soldier, Daddy?"

Dad hugged Richard and rubbed his knuckles on the top of his head. "I have three children to care for and I'm doing very important government work. They wouldn't take me."

"But you can run fast. They need soldiers who can run fast."

"I don't think running fast is very important any more. The fighting is being done in airplanes and tanks."

"And U-boats," Claire added. "Petey Merino saw them in the newsreels. He told me they sank passenger boats. Everybody died. The water was all full of blood, but he said you couldn't tell it was blood because it was black and white."

Dad winced. "I understand that you're concerned, kids, but I wish you would leave the worrying to me." Dad picked Stephen up, holding him under his arms high in the air, and rubbing noses. "Hey, Stevie Stevedore."

Richard rolled onto his back, stuck his legs into the air, and pedaled as if riding an upside-down tricycle. "When is Mom gonna get up? I don't like Claire's cooking."

"Your sister is doing a wonderful job, Richard, cooking, cleaning, doing the wash, taking care of the baby, reading you stories. We're very grateful to her for all she does and I wish to heck she didn't have to do any of it."

This was the opening Claire had hoped for. "Dad, I need to talk to you, about Stephen, and school."

Dad frowned. "I know. Later, Bug. Okay?" He laid Stephen down on his blanket and got to his feet. "I think maybe it's time your mother came downstairs. She can sit out here in the lawn chair and I'll fix some hot dogs for lunch. You two wait here, okay?"

He headed for the house at a run. A cloud passed over the sun, putting Dad in shade. For a minute Claire thought he was a soldier, like in the newsreels, running into battle. She grabbed her throat in terror, waiting for the sound of gunfire. A moment later she heard Mom's shrieks through the open window upstairs. What was going on?

"Put me down. I mean it, Charlie. Put me down."

Richard looked at Claire, pleadingly. "Is he hurting Mom?"

"He wouldn't do that."

"Then why is she screaming?"

"I don't know."

Stephen let out a wail. Claire picked him up and walked him around the yard, talking to calm him. Richard trailed behind, holding on to her skirt. "Hey, bunny boy, look. See those pretty flowers? Those are called cosmos. They're my second favorite, after bachelor's buttons. Do you hear the bird up in the tree? That's Mr. Robin. You can tell he's the mister because he has a red tummy. Mrs. Robin has a green tummy. I'm afraid Mr. Robin is trying to tell us it's going to rain soon." The wind was tossing the leaves of the maple tree, turning their paler undersides up. Clouds, white above, gray below, were moving in. "Once, before it rained," she told Stephen, "Petey Merino said the clouds had dirty bottoms." Richard slapped himself on the forehead and laughed. "Mrs. Bienenmald chased him home with a bar of Fels Naphtha. She said she was going to wash his mouth out with soap. Mrs. Merino said it was none of her business."

"I bet Fels Naphtha tastes awful." Richard clutched his throat and gagged.

"I hope we never find out."

Richard laughed. "The old crab's too fat to catch us anyway."

From far off Claire heard the rumble of thunder. Thank goodness she had hung up a load of diapers while Stephen was taking his morning nap. Maybe Dad would hold Stephen so she could take them down.

Dad pushed open the kitchen screen door with his foot. He was carrying Mom like she was a baby. At least Mom had stopped screaming. He carried her over to the green and white lawn chair and set her in it. "Frances, the sunshine will do you good. Just sit there and I'll go fix lunch."

Claire, with Stephen in her arms and Richard at her side, walked slowly toward the chair where Mom sat clutching her upper arms, her eyes shut tight. She wore only a yellow nightgown. Her skin looked kind of yellow, too. When they were a few feet away, Richard nudged Claire. "Is Mommy crying?"

Claire held a finger to her lips. "Just pretend everything's okay."

Richard ducked his head and turned away. "Okay, but it's not," he mumbled, and now he was crying and there was nothing Claire could do to make it better.

* * *

Dad served boiled hotdogs on a slice of white bread, with a jiggle of yellow mustard. "We don't have any buns," he apologized.

"They taste the same," Claire said, glad she hadn't had to fix lunch for once.

"Better than Fels Naphtha," Richard grumbled with a weird smile on his face.

Dad laughed. "I guess I'll have to be satisfied with faint praise. There's fig newtons and canned pears for dessert, if you eat your hotdog." He turned to Mom. "Frances, since you're not eating, would you like to hold Stephen so Claire can eat?"

Mom opened her eyes and looked at Claire and the baby as if they had come from some other planet. "I'm so tired," she said. "Can't you put him in his carriage?"

Dad took the baby from Claire. "I'll just put him on your lap, for a bit. Claire and I will keep an eye on him."

Claire was relieved to see her mother place a hand on Stephen's tummy. When Mom saw how sweet and warm he was, maybe she would want to hold him in her arms.

In the meantime she saw that Richard was glaring at his hotdog as if it were soap. "I'll beat you," she challenged. "And I'll get all the dessert." She grinned at Dad when Richard took the bait. No one said a word about him stuffing his mouth and not quite closing it while he chewed. At least he was eating.

After lunch, Dad carried the plates into the kitchen while Claire took down the diapers and folded them into the basket, casting occasional wary looks at the sky. After folding the last diaper Claire stood studying the clouds bumping up against one another. The air was full of the honey scent of yellow roses and that peculiar odor that came just before rain. Maybe Carl could come over later, while Stephen was asleep, and they could play checkers or do a jigsaw puzzle. Since Dad was home, she could probably play for a little while.

Stephen shrieked. Claire whirled around. He lay face down in the grass next to Mom's chair, kicking and screaming, sounding terrified. She ran to scoop him up. "It's okay, bunny boy. It's okay." He sobbed and shuddered against her shoulder. What had happened? She'd only turned away for a minute.

She looked at her mother, who looked back putting her fingers against her mouth. "I just closed my eyes for a minute."

Dad burst out the back door, letting the screen door slam. "What happened? Are you okay?" He looked at Claire, then at Frances. "I'm sorry. I thought it would be a good idea." His eyes filled with tears. "The baby's fine, Frances. Don't you worry."

Now everybody was crying. *Mom, Dad, Stephen, Richard. Everybody but me. I am not going to cry,* Claire vowed. *Not not not.*

"Come on, Frances, honey. I'll take you upstairs and get you back in bed."

Claire watched her father gently pick up her mother and carry her into the house. "Come on, Richard, let's go inside," she called.

She fed Stephen his formula, changed him, and tucked him into the carriage. She got a coloring book and crayons for Richard and settled him at the kitchen table, promising him milk and more cookies when she finished the dishes, wondering how she would get everything done. Dad was still upstairs with Mom, but at least they were talking and Mom wasn't crying.

The rain moved in like a silver curtain, batting at leaves, pummeling the flowers, drenching everything in its path. Claire looked out through the kitchen window from her stepstool. The mulberry tree swayed in the wind. The laundry basket, full of folded diapers, sat out under the clothesline in a brown puddle. She couldn't do anything right.

Claire bowed her head and wept.

Chapter
8

laire and Dad fixed the simple dinner together. Mom was
asleep upstairs, exhausted by her short stay outdoors. *It
doesn't make sense,* Claire thought. *Dad carried her
downstairs, left her in a chair, and then carried her back upstairs.
How could that tire someone out? Having a baby must be a really
dangerous thing.*

At least Stephen was dozing in his carriage in the living room,
none the worse for wear for his fall, though Claire's knees quivered
when she thought of what might have happened. The only good
thing was that the rain had stopped almost as soon as it began.

Claire put the string beans she'd bought from Mr. Nishida in the
colander and ran cold water over them. She heard the washing machine chugging away down in the basement, rhythmically washing
diapers for the second time that day. "Wouldn't it be neat if there
was a machine, like a washing machine, only it dried the clothes?
That would be like magic." Not that she much believed in magic
these days. Cinderella was for babies.

Dad set the potato peeler on the counter and hugged Claire, hoot-
ing with delight. "What a wonderful idea. I'm going to invent
one. I'll call it the 'Claire Bug Walters Infernal Clothes Drying
Machine.' We'll make a fortune selling them. New bicycles for
everyone in Marlsburg."

Claire shrugged with sudden happiness. She had made Dad
laugh and she had had a wonderful idea. "When will that be?"

Dad picked up a paring knife and began cutting potatoes into a
pot of water. "Depends on how long my work is needed to help the
Allies. I'm pretty much going to have to continue working seven

days a week for the duration."

That sounded like forever. "What's the 'duration,' exactly?"

Dad shook some salt into the pot and set the pot on the stove. "Basically, it means as long as something lasts. In this case, as long as the war in Europe lasts. But it doesn't have to be about wars. It could be about the duration of a baseball game or a movie. Unfortunately, most of us are thinking about that word in the context of war right now."

That stupid war again. "How long do wars last usually?"

"Good question. Some go on for a long time. The Hundred Years' War lasted a hundred and sixteen years. The War of the Roses ran, on and off, for thirty-two." Dad smiled. "The Great War lasted a little over four years. We were only in it for about a year and a half."

"How come you know so much about wars, Dad?"

For a moment he didn't answer, looking out through the kitchen window as if seeing something that wasn't there, something like a really good dream. "When I was in high school I wanted to be a history teacher, but there wasn't any money for college. I had to go to work, to help make ends meet."

"Because of the Depression." Claire finished snipping off the bean ends and put the beans in a pot with a piece of bacon and some chopped scallions, the way Mrs. Goehner had shown her.

"That's the villain." Dad struck a match and lit the gas stove. "A lot of us didn't get to go to college. After your mother and I got married, I took some correspondence engineering courses. I like engineering well enough, and I can still read history in my spare time, what there is of it."

Claire wiped her hands on a towel. "At least you had today off, even if you had to do work around the house." How she wished Dad could have taken the day just for fun, maybe go to the beach and collect shells, or watch the sandpipers play tag with the waves.

Dad took the towel from her, wiped his hands, and then play-swiped at her legs with it, not enough to sting. "Mr. Berg knows I have some things to take care of right now, so I can keep my mind on what I'm doing at work."

"Like Stephen."

"Like Stephen and you and Richard," he said. "And Mom. My boss knows I've been especially concerned about you."

"Why me, Dad? I'm doing fine and I love taking care of Stephen." She bowed her head, close to tears. Why wasn't she good enough? "You said I was doing a good job."

"You are, Honey. You've done a splendid job of doing everything, but you're a little girl still and school begins in a week and a half. Richard starts kindergarten and you'll be in fourth grade. I know you and Carl have been looking forward to being in Mrs. Bell's class."

True, but things had changed. What if Mom didn't take good care of Stephen? Sometimes she got really mad. Most of the time she was asleep. "Couldn't I stay home? Just until Mom gets better?" she pleaded. "Stephen's used to me. I know what he likes and I tell him stories, and take him for walks...."

Dad pulled out a kitchen chair and sat down. He drew Claire down onto his lap. "You have to go school, Claire. It's the law, and it's the right thing to do. In the future a girl's education is going to be more important than it was in the past. Maybe you'll be an engineer, too. We already have one lady draftsman in our office. You could be a teacher, or a writer, since you love making up stories. Seeing that Stephen is well taken care of is my responsibility. And your mother's, of course."

"But what if he falls again and it's not on the grass? What if he's hungry, or wet, and she doesn't hear him? He'd be so scared. It's not fair, Dad!"

"I *have* thought of that. I spoke to Nana this morning, but she can't come because your grandfather needs her to care for him. By next week, Mom might be just fine." He looked so sad Claire was sure he didn't believe that any more than she did.

"Maybe Mrs. Bell would let me bring Stephen to school. He could sleep in his carriage while I do arithmetic and spelling. During recess I could feed him and change him. I could push him

46

around the schoolyard." She didn't like the grim expression on Dad's face. "It wouldn't be any trouble."

"I can see you've put a lot of thought into this, Claire, and I love you for it, but I'm going to ask Mae Bienenmald to check in during the day," he said, not sounding happy at all.

"Dad, she really is an old crab. Richard was right. And she's mean." Claire twisted around to face him. "She would be a bad influence on Stephen."

The corners of Dad's mouth twitched.

Claire jumped off his lap. "It's not funny, Dad. You don't know what she's like. She says hateful things about Carl and his parents. She says they're krauts and Nazis and that I shouldn't play with Carl." She crossed her arms over her chest. "I love Mrs. Goehner. She helped with Stephen's rash—-it's all gone now--and she's teaching me how to cook. She's the kindest person in the whole wide world."

"I know she is, Claire, and I apologize. I wasn't laughing at you. It's just that I'm not used to having my little girl suddenly be such a big girl, concerned about serious things, and it took me by surprise." He held out his hand. "Forgive me? Pretty please with bananas on my head?" He grinned and made a funny face.

She couldn't hold back an answering smile. She loved him so. "Okay. Just this once," she said, teasing him back.

"Please understand that I don't have too many options. I have to go to work tomorrow. I have to get things with you kids settled before school starts, even if it's not perfect." He stood up and held her against him. "Even if it's Mrs. Bienenmeany."

Claire giggled and hugged him back. Now she really believed he understood what she meant. "Could you just wait until tomorrow to talk to her, please, Dad? I have an idea." She looked up at him and tried to smile again, but her eyes filled with hot tears. "Please." She'd go over first thing in the morning and talk to Carl's mother about Stephen. Mrs. Goehner might know what to do. She might even offer to take care of him until Claire got home from school.

Dad pressed his lips together and nodded. "Okay. Tomorrow."

"Charlie!"

Dad's face brightened. "It's your mother. I'm coming, Franny. Be right there."

"Who left this dirty diaper in the toilet?"

At the stricken look on Dad's face, Claire gulped, "Me. I did. I forgot all about it."

Dad held up his hands. "I'll take care of it, Claire. You can't do everything."

Claire turned away, heartbroken by the change in Dad's face, and saw that the pot of potatoes was boiling over. She ran to the stove to turn down the heat.

* * *

Stephen woke up about four in the morning. Claire groaned. It was so nice and warm in bed, but so far he was only whimpering. Before he could start a full-fledged howl, she switched on her bedside light and got out of bed. She carried him downstairs, hoping the diapers hung in the basement were dry. They were still damp, so she pinned a pair of tea towels on him, glad Nana, who had embroidered them, wouldn't know what she had done. She draped some of the diapers over the oven door. When Dad got up she'd ask him to turn the oven on.

While the bottle heated in a pan of water, she held Stephen and talked to him. "I'm going to dress you in your blue rompers that you look so cute in and take you to talk to Mrs. Goehner." She held him near the window, looking at those blue eyes fastened on hers, and thought he looked too wise to be only a baby, as if an old man were trapped in his little body, an old man worried about something. War probably. The thought scared her for a minute, but soon the bottle was ready and Stephen went back to being a hungry baby.

About six-thirty Dad came down the stairs whistling. "Milkman came early today. 'Milkman, keep those bottles quiet,'" he sang. He went outside to get the milk and stored the bottles in the refrigerator. "Do you want the carriage outside?"

48

"Yes, please, Dad. I'm going to take him for a walk." A very important walk. She could hardly wait.

After a quick breakfast of grape juice and corn flakes, Dad hurried out to the garage. Tuesday was his day to drive.

While Richard stuffed cinnamon toast into his mouth, Claire gave Stephen a sponge bath and dressed him. She took his soft ivory-handled brush and smoothed his hair. "You're my good bunny boy."

There was a sweet tart smell to the air, like apple juice, when she walked outside to lay him in his carriage. She took a deep breath. The sky was a pure blue, as if the rain had washed it clean. Birds called and darted through the air. Bees and butterflies visited flowers. A perfect day. For the first time since Mom came home, Claire felt hopeful.

Richard stumbled out through the kitchen door. "Where're you going?" he asked through a mouthful of toast.

"Goehners'."

"Can I come? She might have strudel." Richard put his head back and smiled at the sky. "Yum."

"Not in your pajamas."

Richard looked down and laughed. "Oh, yeah." He hit himself in the forehead with his hand. "Wait for me. I can run fast." Halfway to the door, he turned around and looked sheepish. "The toast was very delicious."

Richard was trying, she had to admit. "But strudel's better."

"Yeah." He turned to go, then stopped. "Can Joe go, too?"

Claire stifled a smile. "If he's quiet."

"He will be." Richard tore through the kitchen yodeling.

While she waited, impatient to get there, Claire jiggled the carriage. Stephen's eyes opened and closed. "Mrs. Goehner knows what a good baby you are," Claire said. "Everything's going to be just fine."

* * *

As she and Richard pushed the carriage across the street, Petey Merino skated up to them on roller skates, a pair of red wax lips stuck in his mouth. He pulled them out and stuck them in the pocket of his short pants. "Where're you going?"

"None of your beeswax," Claire muttered. "Don't you know it's rude to ask people where they're going?"

"I asked you where you were going," Richard said.

"That's different. You're my brother."

Petey made a face and looked toward the Goehners' house. "Did you hear on the radio that the *Nazis* are in Russia now? Did you hear the *Nazis* are killing thousands of people, not just soldiers? My dad says after they capture all the Russians, the *Nazis* will come here in U-boats because they have friends in New Jersey that will help them. They'll come right up to the shore and climb out of their boats and get us." He held up his hands in a menacing pose.

If Petey said "Nazis" one more time while looking at the Goehners' house, she was going to slap him in the face. "Don't worry, Petey. They wouldn't want you. You're too stupid."

"You're dumb," Petey fired off. He stuck the lips back in his mouth and skated away.

"*He's* dumb," Richard said. "Isn't he? He's lying about the Germans, isn't he?"

"I don't know. Dad doesn't want us to listen to the news any more." Claire wasn't sure if it was better to know what they said on the news, or not to know. What if Petey was right? What if there were Germans in U-boats out near Sandy Hook where Dad worked? What if they came on shore and took *him*? Who would take care of them, with Mom sick and Dad gone? It was more important than ever that she get Mrs. Goehner to help figure everything out.

Claire pushed the carriage up the Goehners' driveway to the back door, half expecting to see Carl's mother working in the garden, but she wasn't there. Mr. Goehner's car was still in the garage. Hadn't he gone to work?

"Go knock on the door, Richard." Claire noticed the row of bottles sitting out in the sun. Why hadn't Mrs. Goehner brought in the milk by now? Pretty soon it would go bad.

Richard walked up to the door and banged on it. "Hello," he called. "Time to get up."

They waited a while, but no one came to the door.

"Maybe someone poisoned them and they all died." Richard stood on tiptoe and peered through the window in the kitchen door.

"Don't be silly."

Richard turned the knob. He looked back at Claire. "It's not locked."

"It's never locked. Close the door. We'll come back later."

"Maybe they're sick and need our help. Come on, Joe." Richard pushed the door open and before Claire could say a word slipped inside.

Claire was sure he'd be back any minute, saying they were in bed or something. She hoped Mrs. Goehner wouldn't be mad when she saw Richard walking through her house.

"Claire!" Richard burst out the door. "There's nobody here. They're all gone."

A flame of fear kindled in Claire's chest. "Maybe they went for a walk or something." Who would go for a walk this early in the morning, except somebody with a baby?

"Joe thinks some of their stuff is gone, maybe," Richard said. "Right, Joe?"

"Right." Richard spoke in a deeper voice without moving his lips.

Claire lifted Stephen from the carriage and settled him on her shoulder. She walked up the steps and into the kitchen. The hair on the back of her neck stiffened. Her legs went numb. She couldn't feel the floor under her feet. The house was cold, like at the bank. "It's so quiet," she whispered.

"Somebody unplugged the refrigerator," Richard said. "That was dumb."

Claire walked through the kitchen into the dining room. Everything looked the same, except the white tablecloth Mrs. Goehner's mother had embroidered was not on the table.

Nothing seemed changed in the living room except the German

clock Mrs. Goehner always kept on the mantel was gone. Richard grabbed hold of her skirt. "See? I told you."

"Did you look upstairs?"

Eyes wide, he nodded. "I'll show you."

They tiptoed up the stairs, scarcely breathing. "Did you look in the closets?" Claire asked.

"Me and Joe didn't think they would be in the closets," Richard said.

Poised in the doorway of the room that was obviously Mr. and Mrs. Goehner's bedroom Claire could only stare. The bed was neatly made as if no one had slept there last night.

"Maybe we should look in the closet," Richard whispered.

"I guess so."

Richard beckoned. "Come on, Joe."

Entering the room Claire felt she was invading some special place, like a church. She opened the closet door. The closet was empty except for a pair of old shoes of Mr. Goehner's and a bath-robe. With a shudder, she closed the door tightly and turned away.

Carl's bed was neatly made as well; his closet empty. Not even a speck of dust like in her closet. "Where did they go?" she whispered, close to tears.

Richard's eyes never left her face. "Maybe the Germans got them and put them in a U-boat and killed them."

Claire remembered the three men in the big black car she had seen coming out of the Goehners' house back before Stephen was born. She'd asked, but Carl would never talk about it. FBI men Petey said they were. "I don't think it was the Germans, Richard." What would FBI men do? Did they take the Goehners away to jail? Why? Maybe the Goehners ran away before the FBI could get them. She hoped they had, but then why hadn't they taken their car?

Stephen let out a piercing scream. He knows something is wrong, Claire thought. "It's okay, bunny boy. We'll go home now."

Once out in the sunshine, he subsided. She was about to set him in the carriage when something made her check under the grape arbor. She almost dropped Stephen when she saw what was there-- Mrs. Goehner's cooking notebook with a note attached.

"For Claire. Remember, my dear girl, if you can read, you can cook. With my affection and respect, Liesl Goehner."

Just below her signature were a few words written in pencil. "Don't forget about me. Your friend, Carl."

* * *

That night Claire dreamed the FBI men had parked their car in front of her house. In the dream, it was the middle of the night. Claire could see a new moon behind wispy clouds. She watched the men get out of the car and approach her house, pointing flashlights at the ground and up to the window where she stood. Gulping fear she ducked behind the curtain. She screamed and screamed to wake her parents, but they slept on. Even Richard wouldn't wake up. At last she grabbed Stephen from his crib and flew down the stairs the way she sometimes could in dreams, as if buoyed by wings. She paused to grab the model rocket Carl had given Stephen, which, for some odd reason, was on top of the refrigerator. She ran into the garden, clutching the baby and the rocket, but in her bare feet she slipped on the wet grass and fell into the Bienenmalds' pond. "Where do you think you're going, little girl?" When she looked up three Nazi soldiers were pointing guns at her. "Give us your puppy," they said. To her horror Stephen had turned into a cocker spaniel. As she reached to hand the soldiers the puppy, she felt someone knocking at her covers as if it were a door.

Suddenly awake, she saw Richard standing by the bed. "I'm scared, Claire," he whimpered.

Me, too, she thought, but didn't say so. Why scare him any more than he already was? "Come on under the covers."

In minutes Richard was asleep, curled into a ball, but Claire lay awake for a long time wondering what had happened to the Goehners.

Chapter
9

Claire and Richard dragged the carriage up the library steps. With each bump, Stephen wailed louder.

"What are you children doing with that baby? Where is your mother?"

Claire waited until the carriage was secure on the top level before answering. She looked up at the scowling red face of Mrs. Roberts, who had been her second grade teacher, but had retired at the end of that year. "Our mother is sick and I'm taking care of him, but I needed to go to the library so Richard's helping me. My dad knows we're doing it."

"Doing what? What's so important at the library you couldn't wait until your mother is well?"

Claire didn't want to tell her. From what she had heard neighbors say, she doubted people would understand. She put a diaper on her shoulder and lifted Stephen out of the carriage. The moment he felt her touch he stopped crying. "Good boy," she whispered against his soft ear.

"Claire's writing a letter to the president," Richard blurted. "We don't know what happened to our neighbors."

Mrs. Roberts' expression softened. "I heard about that. Very strange, them disappearing like that. They seemed like nice people. Apparently appearances are deceiving."

"They *are* nice people." Claire felt her pocket to make sure the pencil and paper were there. "You and Joe watch the carriage, will you, Richard?"

Mrs. Roberts looked around, puzzled. "Joe?"

"My friend," Richard explained with a panicked look at Claire.

"He had to go do something. He'll be right back."

Claire pulled open the door and went inside, pausing a moment to savor the lovely library smell. She walked up to the wide wooden desk piled high with books. Just being around books brought joy to her heart. Mrs. Cunningham, the librarian, sat behind the desk, rolling ink onto a stamp pad.

"Hello, Claire. Is that the new baby?"

Claire felt like saying, no, it's my new puppy, but that would be rude. "This is Stephen. He's two months old today." She turned around to show Mrs. Cunningham his face.

"Make sure he doesn't cry and disturb the patrons."

Claire looked around. The only patron was one old man reading the paper in the corner by the window. "I will."

"He is a cutie."

Claire beamed. "I need to know how to send a letter to the president."

"President Roosevelt? Really? Why?"

Why did grownups always think they could ask you anything, just like it was their business? Claire thought a moment, fishing for an answer that was at least partly true. Probably by now everybody in town knew the Goehners had disappeared, but she didn't want to be the one to spread more stories. No one really knew what had happened, so the stories that went around town were not the truth. Not lies, exactly, either. Just wrong information. If only she knew what the truth was; if only she knew the Goehners were all right. "I want to ask him if we're going to be in a war." She *was* going to ask because, at night when she got in bed, she could scarcely get to sleep, picturing all the U-boats filled with German soldiers just a few miles from shore, like hungry sharks, waiting to land in New Jersey.

"I imagine he's much too busy to read letters from children, but nothing ventured, nothing gained." Mrs. Cunningham stood up, snapped the stamp pad closed, and put the ink roller in a drawer. "Let's go look up that address." She went right to a large book, opened it, and paged through. "This is it. May I hold your little brother while you write down the address?"

"Thank you," Claire said. "Please hold his head so it doesn't wobble."

"I've held babies before," Mrs. Cunningham said, but there was a smile in her voice. "I'll be careful."

Claire copied the address on the piece of paper and stuck it and her pencil back in her pocket. With her fingers she counted the three pennies she'd brought to buy a stamp. After they got home, she would write the letter and give it to the mailman.

* * *

"Dear President Roosevelt,

I am writing you a letter to ask if you know what happened to my friend Carl and his parents. They disappeared one night last week. A boy who lives on my street says the FBI got them. Their names are Mr. and Mrs. Goehner. Here is their address. 416 Atlantic Lane, Marlsburg, New Jersey.

If you can find out if they are all right and how I can write to them, I would be very happy.

My dad says you promised we would not be in the war. I hope that is true.

Yours truly,

Claire Irene Walters
P.S. Carl is an American...

Claire put down her pencil and ran upstairs. "Mom?" she whispered.

Mom groaned but turned toward Claire. "What's the matter now?"

"How do you spell citizen?"

"Can't you ask Daddy?"

"He's at work."

"Is that something for school?"

"School starts next week."

56

Mom spelled the word. "Is that all you need?"

"Yes. Thanks, Mom." She leaned over and gave her mother a kiss. "If you want something to eat, let me know. I can make you a sandwich or some chicken noodle soup."

"Maybe later, Claire. In a little while." Mom made a half smile. "Thank you, though."

Claire sighed happily. Maybe Mom was getting better.

* * *

Claire held Richard's hand as they approached the two story brick schoolhouse. For the first time since starting kindergarten she dreaded going inside. Even the new green and white striped dress Nana had made for her didn't make her feel better. She should be with Stephen.

In the schoolyard she saw her friend, Grace, putting her bicycle in the rack. At least they could talk later. Grace had been in Michigan all summer with her cousins. "Come on," she told Richard. "Let's go find your classroom."

"You don't have to show me. I know where it is," Richard said. "Mom took me there once, before...." He made a face. "Stephen." He took the nickel she gave him for milk and stuck it in the pocket of his new pants. "Come on, Joe," he said in a small voice.

"I thought Dad told you to leave him at home."

Richard's lip quivered. His eyes filled. "He did, but Joe promised to be really really good and not talk."

Poor Richard. He was scared; she could see that. He had been braver before Mom got sick. What difference would it make if Joe went with him? Richard stuck his hands in his pants pockets and gave her a pleading smile, just like the boy in the Campbell soup ads. Claire wanted to hug him, but she knew he'd squawk.

"Okay, Joe. As long as you're quiet and don't slurp Richard's milk."

Richard giggled and turned and galloped down the hall toward the kindergarten room, slapping his thighs and yodeling. Claire watched until he was safely in his classroom thinking it was a good thing Joe would be quiet, because Richard made enough noise for two.

* * *

"I hear you have a new baby," Grace said behind her hand. With her other hand she fluffed up her blond curls, just like the ones Claire used to have, before, when Mom cared how Claire's hair looked. She had made curls by wrapping strands of damp hair in strips of cloth torn from old sheets. Sleeping on rag curlers was uncomfortable, but the results were worth the trouble. Everybody told you how pretty your hair looked. Just like Shirley Temple.

Nobody would say that today. Claire's hair was a mess. Dad had tried his best, but he was better at doing Richard's hair. If Nana saw her, she'd say Claire looked like the wrath of God. Whatever that was. At least her socks matched her dress.

Mrs. Bell had just passed out arithmetic worksheets—-long column addition, "To see how much you boys and girls remember from third grade." Pretending she was a contestant in an addition contest Claire got to work. If she finished all three pages by nine-thirty, she would win first prize, a blue bike with balloon tires and a pink straw basket in the front. She was good at arithmetic. Maybe she *would* be an engineer, but she'd rather design houses.

The classroom windows were open, letting in playground dust, the smell of drying leaves, and the shrieks of jays. Their cries sounded different in the fall, as if they were upset that summer was over. Almost as upset as she was. Was Stephen all right? Mom had said she'd watch him, but Claire wasn't so sure. What if she had put him on the bed and he fell off onto the hard floor? He would be so scared. And probably hurt. In her mind she heard him sobbing and could scarcely stand the thought.

She put down her pencil and took a quick look around. Mrs. Bell was arranging supplies in the storage closet while all the kids bent over their long column addition, except Petey Merino who was shooting rubber bands out the window. Claire got up from her chair.

"Where're you going?" Grace whispered.

"Girls room. I'm gonna be sick." Claire bolted out of the classroom. The slap of her oxfords on the marble floor echoed in the hall. As she burst through the front door, Mrs. Clough, the school secretary, yelled, "Stop," but Claire ran on. If anything had happened to Stephen, she'd never forgive Dad for making her go to school.

She felt as if she were swimming in deep water, as if she would never get there, as if she would drown in fear. Sunlight and shade and the first falling yellow leaves of autumn left her dizzy. Please let him be all right. She turned onto Atlantic Lane, pausing for a moment to catch her breath. Ignoring the stitch in her side, she ran again.

"Where are you going, young lady?" Mrs. Bienenmald stopped sweeping her front walk to shake a finger at Claire. "You should be in school."

Claire swept on by, not caring if she was rude. She'd apologize later, but only if Dad made her. She yanked open the front door and ran inside, her heart a jackhammer in her chest. She looked in the carriage in the living room. Stephen wasn't there. She tore up the stairs to Mom and Dad's room where they'd moved the bassinet, even though Dad knew it broke her heart to have him out of her room.

Mom was sitting up in bed, wearing a blue bed jacket. Her hair was held away from her face with combs. Sun streamed in through the open windows, making moving patterns of light and dark on the pink chenille spread. Mom smiled wanly. "Claire. What are you doing here?"

Claire gasped and collapsed face down on the bed. "I was so worried, Mom. In case Stephen needed me. Or you did." Claire felt Mom's hand stroking her hair once, twice. She wanted to lie there forever, but the hand pulled away.

"Mrs. Bienenmald's been in. She fed Stephen and gave him his bath. She had to go home, but she'll be back at lunch time."

That was the most Mom had said since she came home with the new baby. Claire rubbed her eyes with her knuckles and stood up, smoothing her dress. "Can I get you anything while I'm here?"

"No, I'm not hungry. You should go back to school."

"I will." Claire walked around the bed and hugged her mother, then stopped to touch Stephen's cheek. "See you later, bunny boy." She turned to wave to her mother, but Mom's eyes had already closed. She left the room and went downstairs, dragging her feet.

As she left the house her eyes were drawn to the Goehners' house. Why wasn't Carl there anymore? Why couldn't he go to fourth grade with her? Where were his parents? Maybe Carl would send her a letter and tell her where he was. Maybe they'd come back and say they had just been on a little vacation.

"Just what in the name of all that's holy are you doing home in the middle of the morning?" Mrs. Bienenmald, still clutching her broom, blocked out the light of the sun.

"I came to make sure my mother was all right. And the baby."

"I suppose you think I'm not capable of taking care of a baby." The woman's voice sounded like a snake hissing. She grabbed Claire's shoulder and shook her. "Answer me, young lady."

"I'm sure you are," Claire said, knowing she was lying again, "but, you see, I love Stephen." And you don't. "That's the difference."

Mrs. Bienenmald huffed. "Well, that's the most ridiculous thing I've ever heard."

Claire tried to shrug away from the painful, digging fingers, but Mrs. Bienenmald held tight.

"I saw you looking across the street at those people's house. Don't you wonder where those Nazis went? Back to Germany, I bet."

Claire bit her lip to keep from saying something that would get her in more trouble than she already was.

"Well, good riddance to bad rubbish, I always say." At last she let go of Claire's shoulder. "You need to get yourself back to school, missy. You're going to be in a lot of trouble. Yes, indeed. A peck of trouble."

"I was on my way back," Claire said.

"A likely story." Mae Bienenmald grabbed Claire's right earlobe between her thumb and forefinger. "Someone needs to keep an eye on you, Sister Sue, getting too big for your britches. Your daddy sure isn't. Now march!"

No one had ever pinched Claire on the earlobe. Astonished at how much it hurt, she was humiliated as Mrs. Bicncnmald strode toward the school, dragging Claire with her. *I will never in my life do this to a child when I'm grown up.*

Mrs. Clough wasn't at her desk in the school office. "Where's your classroom?" Mrs. Bienenmald demanded, giving a sharp yank to Claire's earlobe, in case she hadn't heard.

Claire pointed down the hall, fighting to keep the tears out of her voice. "Room 4. Mrs. Bell."

"Missus? A married teacher! I never heard of such a thing! What next?"

"She's a widow. Her husband died. She has to work. She's a good teacher."

"Well, if she's a widow, that's better, I guess. It still doesn't seem right."

How could being a widow be better? "Mr. Hathaway, the principal, is married." Claire tried to twist away from Mrs. Bienenmald's pinching thumb and finger, but couldn't.

"That's different. He's a man."

How could that be different? Grownups were certainly strange sometimes. Maybe it was just Mrs. Bienenmald who was strange.

The classroom was empty. Through the open windows Claire could see the kids out on the playground, girls jumping rope, boys playing kickball or tag.

Mrs. Bienenmald marched Claire back down the hall and out onto the playground. Mrs. Bell, in her soft brown dress and brown and white pumps, started toward them. Her face flamed.

"Claire. What's the matter?"

"I caught her sneaking home," Mrs. Bienenmald snapped. "And brought her back where she belongs." She gave another tug to Claire's earlobe.

All the kids stopped their games to turn and stare. Claire's cheeks flushed with shame.

"You can let go of her now," Mrs. Bell said, tightlipped, her eyes flashing anger.

"Is that all the thanks I get?" Mrs. Bienenmald wheeled around and clomped off, fists tight, elbows pumping.

Mrs. Bell led Claire over to a picnic table. "Sit down, Claire." She swung a pointing finger at the kids. "Go back to your activities, class." She sat down next to Claire. "Grace said you were sick."

Claire shook her head. "I didn't tell her the truth, Mrs. Bell. I lied." She rubbed at her burning earlobe.

Mrs. Bell put a gentle hand on Claire's back. "I'll bet you had a good reason."

The tears Claire had stifled for so long flowed out. After a minute or two Mrs. Bell pulled a tissue from her sleeve. "Here, Claire. Mop up."

At last Claire could speak. "My mother had a baby this summer, but she's been sick. I'm not supposed to talk about it, because it's not nice, but she has the baby blues and she sleeps all the time, so I had to take care of Stephen. He's the baby. He's a really good baby." She smiled then. "When I was doing the long column addition, I started to worry because he's home with just my mother and I don't know if she'll wake up if he's hungry or wet and Dad had to go to work and Mrs. Bienenmald...." She glared in the direction the woman had taken. "She's mean. I don't want her taking care of Stephen. She said good riddance to bad rubbish because the Goehners disappeared."

Mrs. Bell nodded. "That's disturbing, isn't it? I was expecting Carl to be in my class. No one knows what happened?"

"No, but Carl's mother isn't rubbish. She helped me all summer. She showed me how to cook supper and take care of Stephen's rash and gave me lots of stuff from her garden. She left me her cookbook, so I don't think she's ever coming back." Claire looked up into Mrs. Bell's face and saw only kindness. "I wrote to President Roosevelt to see if he knows where the Goehners are, because

Petey said there were FBI men in their house."

"Oh, dear. Goodbye civil liberties," Mrs. Bell muttered.

"What does that mean, Mrs. Bell?"

"It means sometimes the government does stupid and illegal things in wartime. Laws fly out the window and ordinary people pay the price."

"Do you think the Goehners disappeared because we might get in the war?"

"I have no idea about that, Claire. It's possible." Mrs. Bell sighed. "I do think there's a good chance we'll have to go overseas to help the Allies. My son is in the Navy, over in Hawaii. I worry about him every minute of every day."

"What's his name?"

"Stephen. Isn't that a funny coincidence? I guess we both have our Stephens to worry about. You can let me know how things are going with your Stephen."

"You, too," said Claire. The passing bell rang. "I *was* coming back to school. Honest."

"I believe you." Mrs. Bell stood up. "Time to go in, boys and girls. Are you all right now, Claire?"

She wasn't sure. "Sort of."

"Sometimes that's the best you can hope for." She patted Claire's shoulder and walked toward the door. "Okay, children, line up, please."

As Claire took her place at the end of the girls' line she promised herself that she would worry about Stephen Bell, too. Nobody as nice as Mrs. Bell should have to worry alone.

Sunday, Nov. 23, 1941

Chapter
10

Claire's ninth birthday fell on a Sunday. For a week now Mom had been spending an hour or two a day downstairs in her rocking chair paging through a magazine, or dozing. Claire and her father were still doing the cooking, but just having Mom nearby made the job seem easier. As usual, Dad was at work but he had promised to try to get home a little earlier than usual. Sometimes, on Sundays, the men drove their own cars and left when they were done working.

For her eighth birthday, the year before, Claire had invited Grace and Carl over for cake and chocolate ice cream. *Carl's been gone for three whole months*, she thought. *Gone where?* The furniture and Mr. Goehner's car had been sold and taken away. A new family was moving in in a week or so. How did they know where to send the Goehners the money from selling the house and furniture if no one knew where they were? *Somebody must know*, Claire thought, even though President Roosevelt still had not replied to her letter to tell her. Mrs. Cunningham had been right. A President didn't have time to read letters from children.

Claire went to the front window and looked out, wishing with all her heart that she would see Carl waving from his window. But his blue curtains were gone, the windows dark, making her think of the eyes in an unlit jack o'lantern. Scary. She watched the trees shiver in the wind. Only a few yellow leaves still clung tight to the branches. It was her favorite kind of day, with gray skies and the promise of snow—-the kind of day when you were glad to stay inside, drink hot cocoa, and read or play paper dolls. Maybe Grace could come over later.

Richard joined her at the window. "Are you gonna have a birthday cake?"

She shrugged as if it didn't matter. "Probably not."

"You could make one."

"I've never made a cake in my whole life."

"I'll help," Richard said. "Mommy likes cake."

Claire decided a cake was a good idea. *If you can read, you can cook*, Mrs. Goehner had told her. "Maybe I can find a recipe for something easy." Claire searched through Mom's card file, but all the recipes were for two layer cakes. "These would be too hard. A cake that's just one layer and you don't have to take it out of the pan, that's what we need, but I can't find one." Richard looked so disappointed, she tried to think of another way to make cake. Maybe she could look in Mrs. Goehner's cooking notebook. She ran upstairs and got the notebook from her dresser drawer where she kept it. Behind the book she saw the ring Carl had given her. She picked it up and slipped it over her thumb. Still too big. *Where are you, Carl?* She put the ring back in the drawer, pushing it all the way to the back and covering it with a pair of socks she didn't like.

Downstairs she opened the notebook on the kitchen table and paged through it. She could scarcely make out the names of anything from Mrs. Goehner's funny handwriting. As she turned more pages, an envelope fell out. The stamp had "Deutschland" on it. Was that the German word for Holland, or did it mean Germany? The handwriting on the envelope was even swirlier than Mrs. Goehner's. Claire wondered who the letter was from...maybe Carl's grandmother, the one he called "Oma."

Finally she came to a recipe cut from the Marlsburg newspaper for a one-egg one-pan cake. "We'll try this one."

Claire had watched Mom make things often enough to know that you measured half a cup of butter by putting half a cup of water into the measuring cup and adding butter until the water reached the one cup line. As she added ingredients to the big yellow and tan bowl, she gave instructions to Richard. "Okay, stir the butter with the sugar until it's all mixed really well." Once that was done, she cracked the egg into the bowl. A piece of shell fell in. "Richard, wait. I'll get that out with a spoon."

Richard let out a sigh.

"It'll only take a second."

"I know." Richard bowed his head and looked away.

"Okay. You can stir now."

Richard let go of the wooden spoon and stared into the bowl. When his shoulders slumped, Claire could see something more than a piece of eggshell was bothering him. She put a hand on his back the way Mrs. Bell had done on hers the first day of school because she remembered how good it had felt. She didn't know what to say except, "What is it, Richard?"

He turned to look at her, his mouth turned down, his eyes sad. "Well, if we have to do all the work, well...you do most of it... well...oh, never mind."

"Well what?"

Richard picked up the wooden spoon and began stirring the cake ingredients, but Claire could see his heart wasn't in it. "Nothing."

What would Mom do? What would Mrs. Goehner say? Claire wasn't sure, but she tried. "It's not nothing if it's bothering you. So out with it! If we have to do all the work...what? We should get more allowance? You already get a nickel a week, same as me. You should get more stars on your chores chart? You shouldn't have to go to school anymore?"

"I like kindergarten," Richard protested.

"Richard, I am not a mindreader." That's what Mom would say.

Richard dropped the spoon again, crossed his arms over his chest, and pursed his lips. He looked so much like Dad Claire was startled. Everyone always said Richard favored Mom's side of the family.

"I don't want to be Richard anymore," he said. "I'm a big boy. I go to school now and I do a lot of work."

"So who do you want to be?"

He looked down, twisted his mouth, looked up. "Dick. Like in

Dick and Jane. See Dick run. I bet they don't ever call him Richard, do they? What a dumb name."

So that was it! Claire kept her face straight. "I never heard of him being called anything but 'Dick.' That's going to be hard to remember, but I'll try." She put her hands on his cheeks, making him look at her. "Dick."

Richard beamed. "Will you tell Daddy? And Mommy? To call me Dick? Not Dicky either, like Dicky Helstrom. Just Dick."

"Sure." She hugged him. "And Nana."

"And my teacher?" he asked hopefully.

"I think maybe Dad will have to do that."

Richard chuckled. "Then all the kids will have to call me Dick, too, won't they, just like I'm a big boy? 'Cause I am now."

"If they remember."

"Not a big boy who has to be in the Army. Not that big."

"Not in the Army. Just kindergarten." She smiled. "Dick."

He smiled back and then looked out the window. She thought he was probably imagining what it would be like when he went back to school the next day and would be Dick, not Richard. A big boy. Not a big boy who has to be in the Army, thank goodness. Would there still be a war when he was eighteen?

Why did there have to be wars anyway? She didn't want Mrs. Browne's son, Warren, to be in the war. He was nice. She didn't even want Mrs. Bienenmald's grandson to be in the war. It wasn't his fault his grandmother was a mean old witch.

But what could she do? Had the president lied, just so he could get elected again? But how could the president of the United States lie? Wasn't a president almost kind of like God?

She would write him another letter. He probably wouldn't read it anyway. No one ever paid attention to kids, especially if they were girls.

Chapter
11

Frances Walters' birthday came two weeks after Claire's, also falling on a Sunday. Claire found a recipe in the Marlsburg paper for another one-pan cake, called Pineapple Upside Down Cake. It was easy to make and for once they had all the ingredients so they wouldn't have to wait for Dad to come home from work and take them to the store.

She set Stephen in his high chair, since he could now sit up very well, and gave him some zwieback to chew on. The recipe called for four pineapple slices set in the bottom of the pan and five cherries, four of which were to be placed in the center of each pineapple slice, and one to go in the middle. Richard...Dick, Claire reminded herself...was given the task of laying the pineapple slices on top of the brown sugar and butter and adding the cherries. He ignored the pictured pattern and stuck cherries everywhere he found room. "Mommy loves cherries," he explained. After he finished, he drank the juice from the jar. When he began popping the remaining cherries into his mouth, one at a time, Stephen cried so bitterly Claire said, "Dick, give two to the baby, one for each hand. You have to share."

Stephen sobbed, hiccoughed, smiled, and gummed the cherries, all the while gazing at Claire with total adoration.

"You're my bunny boy," she told him.

"Then who am I?" Dick demanded, looking hurt.

It wasn't easy with kids, was it? she thought. "You're the big boy who helped make Mom's cake and did such a good job arranging the cherries. You're Dick."

He nodded, proud and happy, and took another cherry from the jar. He placed it on Stephen's highchair tray with a flourish. "You can have the last one." Claire heard him whisper, "Baby!" but let it go. At least he had shared.

Once the cake came out of the oven, had partially cooled, and been overturned onto a cake plate, Claire took a clean dishcloth and wiped Stephen's hands and face, sticky from clots of zwieback and red with cherry juice. "I'm taking Stephen for a walk," she called to Mom, who was sitting in her rocking chair in the living room, listening to the radio. Mom didn't answer, but she often didn't.

Claire dressed Stephen in his tan tweed coat and matching cap, a hand-me-down from Richard. The coat was a little big, but he looked adorable in it anyway. "You want to go...Dick?"

Dick shook his head. "Joe and I are going to play checkers," he explained with a grin wreathed in cherry juice. "I always win." He shrugged with pride.

"No cheating," she teased.

"I don't have to cheat. Joe's not very good." He put his hands on his hips. "Sometimes he just doesn't pay attention."

He sounded so much like Mom used to, Claire didn't know whether to laugh or cry. She did neither. When she thought about it, it wasn't funny enough to laugh about and she didn't want to cry. Once she started she might never stop.

She tied a light blue wool kerchief over her braids and slipped on her navy coat from last year. The sleeves were a little short and the shoulders tight. Maybe Nana would make her a new one for Christmas if she asked nicely. "If Dad comes home before I get back, tell him where I am."

The day was mild for early December, but overcast with a hint of dampness in the air. Claire started in the direction of the school, intending to circle the playground and come back. A couple of boys from Dick's class were playing on one of the seesaws behind the school. Just beyond the schoolyard Claire saw a young woman raking leaves. She looked twice when she saw the woman was wearing pants, like a man. When you thought about it, pants made sense. If girls could wear them to school, when they hung from the jungle gym they wouldn't have to hold their dresses up so no one could see their underpants. Of course everybody saw them anyway, so you never wore old ones to school.

I'll go just one more block, Claire decided, but when she reached the corner, she saw that Stephen had fallen asleep. Nana said fresh air was good for babies. She kept going. Now she was in a neighborhood she didn't know well. The houses were small, one story mostly, with tiny but well-kept lawns, all brown now. Mom's friend, Marian, lived around here somewhere. Yes. In that white house with black trim around the windows down at the corner.

Nobody came to see Mom anymore. Claire was tempted to knock on Marian's door but how would it sound if she said, "How come you don't come to see my mother anymore?" She knew why anyway. Mom scarcely noticed the people who came and finally they shrugged and went away, promising to be back another day when poor Frances was feeling more like her old self again.

Claire thought she should turn around, but it was so good to be out of that gloomy house, away from dirty clothes and dirty dishes and dirty floors. Dirty diapers. What freedom to have nothing to do but walk and look at houses. She loved the one they were just passing, made of tan bricks with the swooping roofline over the door. If she had been the architect, she would have made the windows bigger. The ones in the front with the shades half drawn made the house look cross.

She amused herself as she pushed the carriage farther from home, redesigning houses, rearranging their windows and doors, lifting a roof, or adding a screened porch until she came to where the pavement ended. She knew she should go home, but something drew her down the treelined dirt road she had never been on. She saw that the houses were farther apart on that stretch of road and had fruit trees in their yards with here an apple, there a cherry that the birds had somehow missed, brown and dried up, still hanging from the branches.

When she came to the end of the road where a thicket of bushes screened the property beyond, Claire saw she had no choice but to turn back. But she had glimpsed a building and reached to pull the branches aside and peer through them for a better look. She saw a dwelling unlike any she had ever seen before. Made of plain wood, weathered to a soft gray-brown, the house had a sloping roof that hung out from the sides like the sun hat Mr. Nishida wore when he delivered his fruits and vegetables in the summer. The effect was peaceful and inviting, like a cottage a fairy godmother would build. What lucky duck lived in that beautiful place?

She noticed the frost-killed garden beyond the house, laid out in neat rows like Mrs. Goehner's. Past a row of fruit trees she saw a weathered barn with a Dutch door. The bottom half was closed and, as she stood there, a horse stuck its head through the open upper part and looked around. Momoko.

Claire whispered, "This must be Mr. Nishida's house." So this was where he lived and grew his vegetables and fruit. Once last summer she had asked him if she could visit his house and help him with the garden. "If it's all right with your mother," he had said, or something like that. The day had never come because Claire had been busy with Stephen. Maybe he would remember and be glad to see her.

"Come on, Stephen," she said to her sleeping brother. "Let's go say hello." Eagerly she maneuvered the carriage through a break in the bushes. Chickadees twittered as they passed. The carriage wheels crunched on the gravel path. Claire parked the carriage by the front door and set the brake. She looked for a doorbell but, seeing none, knocked gently.

After only a moment, the door opened. A tiny lady who looked a little like Mr. Nishida studied Claire with raised eyebrows. "Yes?" She smoothed the front of her blue and gray housedress.

Claire felt herself blush. "I thought, I mean, does Mr. Nishida live here? I was out walking and I saw your house...it's so beautiful...and once he said I could visit, but that was a long time ago. I'm sorry to disturb you. I saw Momoko and thought maybe this was his house."

"Are you Claire?" the woman asked with a smile.

"How did you know?" Maybe the little lady was a fairy god-mother if she knew who Claire was.

"Please come in. We are in the kitchen. My brother will be happy to see you and the baby."

Stephen woke up when Claire lifted him from the carriage, but he appeared quite content. He stared with big eyes at the unfamiliar place, seemingly as fascinated as Claire.

As she led Claire through the main room, the woman added, "My brother has spoken of you often. What a help you are to your mother."

How did he know that, Claire wondered.

"Paul, you have visitors," the lady said as they entered the small kitchen. Dark blue curtains with white flower designs on them hung from a wooden curtain rod. On the drainboard, next to the sink, lay a white vegetable, like an enormous radish. The lady picked up a flowered apron from the back of one of the chairs and put it on. She took a large knife from a drawer and began slicing the giant radish.

Mr. Nishida looked up and smiled broadly when he saw Claire. His eyes almost disappeared in the crinkles of skin. "Well, you are a long way from home, young lady." He set down the piece of wood he had been carving and held out his hands. "Will he come to me?"

"He'd better," Claire said, joking. "Since you're being so nice to invite us in." Stephen went right to Mr. Nishida without a sound.

"Would you like some tea? It's green tea, from Japan," Mr. Nishida's sister said.

"I've never had any kind of tea before, but I'd like to try some. Thank you." Claire loved that Mr. Nishida's sister offered her tea, as if she were a grownup visitor.

Mr. Nishida undid the snap on Stephen's cap and laid the cap on the table. He unbuttoned the little tweed coat and pulled it off so gently Stephen didn't even fuss the way he usually did. "My sister's name is Rose," Mr. Nishida said, making faces at Stephen.

"Hello, Mister Stephen." Stephen laughed and tried to grab Mr. Nishida's glasses. "Oh, no, you don't, you rascal."

Rose poured tea from a dark iron pot into a tiny cup with no handles. Claire found the pink flowers painted on the side enchanting. The tea didn't smell like the kind Nana drank, and didn't look the same. Claire was sure she would like it, but how did you hold the cup?

"This way," said Rose, as if she had read Claire's mind. Cradling her own cup in two hands she took a small sip. She set down her cup and pushed a plate of tiny pink wafers toward Claire. "You might not like these, but please try one anyway." She turned to her brother. "We may not get more for a while, so you had better enjoy them, too." She turned back to Claire. "They aren't shipping things from Japan right now. It's very worrisome."

Claire studied the woman's face. Her skin was a lovely golden tan, her features flat and delicate, her eyes hooded. She had a pointed chin and a broad forehead, so that her face was shaped like an acorn. Claire turned away for a moment, listening to brother and sister talk. They sounded like anybody else in town. If she hadn't known what they looked like she would expect them to look like members of her family or a neighbor. Why did people look different and speak different languages? Why did it matter to some people? God must have meant for people to be as different as flowers in the garden, or maybe as different as vegetables, since vegetables were more useful, but still, it was odd. Kind of like wondering about stars and where the universe ended.

"Why aren't they shipping?" Claire asked politely, after a sip of the pale yellow tea. She wasn't sure she liked the taste, but the cup was small. She could certainly be polite and finish the drink.

"Because they are building warships and saving the fuel they have for the warships," Rose said angrily. "Some people in the government of Japan want war. They want to conquer Asia. They have already invaded China and they want to fight us, too. If there is war, I am afraid it will be bad for Paul and me, even if we were born here and went to school in Marlsburg."

"Because you look Japanese even though you're not. Not exactly." Claire took another sip from the delicate little cup. "My friend Carl and his parents disappeared last summer. They don't look at all different, but Carl's parents were born in Germany and talk a little funny. Mrs. Bienenmald says they were spies. She hopes they were put in prison where they couldn't hurt decent people. I hate her."

Mr. Nishida made a rude noise. "I wouldn't sell a dried up apple to Mrs. Bienenmald, if my life depended on it."

"Thankfully it doesn't," Rose commented with a smile.

Claire giggled. She couldn't help it. "I wish she wasn't taking care of Stephen when I'm at school. I wish somebody nice would take care of him until my mother gets well. I was going to ask Mrs. Goehner to help, but she's gone, and somebody sold their house and all their belongings. They'll never come back, I just know it." She pressed her hands against her chest, as if to soften the pain in her heart, but she couldn't stop the tears.

Rose handed her a handkerchief. "We were sorry to hear about that. They were a nice family."

How kind she was. Claire dabbed at her eyes. Maybe Rose could take care of Stephen. Did she dare suggest it?

"Lots of people in this country have German names. It doesn't mean they're spies, although some of them surely are. I guess the government is afraid to take a chance." Mr. Nishida gave Stephen one of the little wafers which he grabbed and began gumming. "That's the boy."

Claire thought that Mr. Nishida and his sister lived far from town. Maybe if they changed their name, nobody would know their parents came from Japan and they wouldn't think they were spies, too, and steal their house. "Does Nishida mean something in English?"

"West field," Rose told her.

Maybe they could call themselves "Westfield." "There's a town named Westfield," Claire said. "Isn't it funny how different kinds of people make their names?"

74

"Japanese names usually come from natural things, like Tanaka, middle field, or Matsunaka, middle pine tree, Oshima, Honorable Island," Rose told her.

"My grandma's name was Baker when she wasn't married to my grandpa. English people used to take their names from what they did. What the husbands did, I mean. I don't know where Walters came from, though." Claire glanced up at the clock on the wall. How had it gotten so late so fast? It would be dark soon. "Oh, my gosh, I'd better get going. No one knows where I am and they might be worried. I'm going to be in so much trouble."

"I'll take you home, Claire." Mr. Nishida quickly put Stephen's cap and coat back on him, stood up, and passed Stephen to Claire. He grabbed a red and black mackinaw from a hook on the back of the door and put it on.

"In the vegetable wagon?"

He laughed. "I have a car. It's only a coupe, but we can put Stephen's carriage in the rumble seat."

Mr. Nishida's car was light green with just two seats in the front and a rumble seat in the back. Claire so wished she could ride in the rumble seat, but they had to put the carriage there. With Stephen clutched tightly to her chest, she waved goodbye to Rose. "See you soon, I hope," she called.

Mr. Nishida drove slowly on the dirt road, but speeded up once they got to pavement.

"Today's my mother's birthday," she told him as they drove past the school. "I made a cake." Would Mom even notice? Remembering how Dick had said, "Mommy loves cherries," she hoped so.

"Please give her my congratulations." Mr. Nishida pulled into the driveway. Claire could see Dad's car through the garage windows. She gulped, hoping Dad wouldn't be mad. What if Dick hadn't remembered to tell him that she was walking Stephen?

Mr. Nishida got out and came around to her side. He opened the door and held Stephen while she got out, then handed him back. While she stood there, he took the carriage out of the rumble seat and set it on the driveway. "I'll go up to the door with you," he said. "Your parents will probably want an explanation."

They hadn't made it to the door when Claire's father came outside. He stood at the top of the steps looking so grim Claire was sure she would be punished, maybe even spanked, even though Dad had never spanked her before, except for a love tap on her birthday.

"Hello, Mr. Walters," Mr. Nishida said. "Your daughter showed up at my door this afternoon...she found us while she was out walking...and, well, it's quite a distance and getting late, so I brought her home. My sister and I enjoyed their visit."

Dad walked down the steps and reached for Stephen. He looked Mr. Nishida in the face. His expression had gone from grim to sad. "The Japanese have bombed Pearl Harbor in Hawaii. Thousands of Americans have been killed. We're in the war now, for sure."

Claire gasped. "Rose was afraid of that, wasn't she?"

Mr. Nishida's face turned so pale she worried he would faint. "So was I." He patted Claire's shoulder. "I had better get home before Rose turns on the radio and hears the news."

Claire's father held out his hand. "We don't hold any grudge against you and your sister, but a lot of Americans died today. I can't speak for my neighbors." His eyes flicked toward the house next door, then back. "Be on the alert."

Mr. Nishida shook Claire's father's hand without another word. He turned then and ran to the car. Moments later he backed out of the driveway and headed up the street, driving faster than before.

"Poor fellow," Dad said, watching until the car was out of sight. "Things may be tough for him."

"Poor Rose, you mean," Claire said, as she pulled the carriage up the steps onto the porch. "That's his sister. She's really nice. I was hoping maybe she could take care of Stephen while I'm at school, instead of...." She made a face and turned to look at the Bienenmalds' house. "Her."

"Claire, that might have been a good idea...before. After what happened today, that's not going to be possible," Dad said. "Come on. Let's go give Mom her present. I bought her a pair of those

Daniel Green slippers she likes. We'd better have some of the cake you made before your brother picks out the rest of the cherries." He laughed, but the laugh sounded more sad than crying.

Claire followed him into the house. Somehow it didn't matter anymore that she'd forgotten to ask him to buy candles. She didn't even care if Dick ate all the cherries off the cake.

As she walked into the living room, her teacher's face came to her mind. *Oh, Mrs. Bell*, she thought, crossing her fingers. *Your son is in Hawaii. I hope your Stephen wasn't one of those Americans who got killed.*

Mother was still in the rocking chair, just as Claire had left her, except that she was crying. More like leaking from the eyes because she didn't make a sound as the tears ran down her face and dripped onto her pink bathrobe. "I knew it," she moaned. "I just knew it. We'll all be killed in our beds."

Dinner was a gloomy time, even though birthday cake was the only thing they ate. Mother wouldn't come to the table or open her present. No one, not even Dick, suggested singing "Happy Birthday."

After she went to bed, Claire tried to get to sleep by making up stories in her head about going dancing in a long golden dress with a man in a navy blue suit, a man who looked a little like Mandrake, the Magician, but all she could think was, *I wonder if Mr. Nishida and Rose will disappear, too. I wonder if Stephen Bell is all right. I wonder if Dad will have to be in the Army.*

The next day a substitute taught fourth grade.

Chapter
12

C laire tied on the red gingham apron Nana had sent Mother for her birthday. "Surely she's cooking for her family now," she told Claire over the phone when she called to make sure the package had arrived. "So you don't have to."

"We take turns." It wasn't really the truth, but Claire hated being in the middle.

Mother rarely made anything but toast, and then complained about the nasty flavor of margarine. She had never been much of a cook anyway. At least in the past six months, Mom had been staying up after supper to listen to the radio, while knitting squares for afghans for the wounded soldiers, and even talking a little with Dad while Claire got the boys tucked in bed.

Claire enjoyed doing the cooking. In the years since the war started, she had learned to piece together tasty meals using leftovers, vegetables from the Victory Garden she and Dick had planted, and the chickens Dad raised. Now, at the holidays, she was determined they would have dessert for Christmas—-pie, Dad's favorite--even if it was mostly raisins.

The Thanksgiving pie had not been a great success. The chicken fat she'd had to use in the crust had overpowered the pumpkin filling even though she'd doubled the spices. They ate it anyway. Dad had somehow procured a pound of lard for Christmas baking, which would be much better.

Dick sat at the table, glumly watching Claire assemble the ingredients for piecrust. "Pies aren't patriotic," he said. "That's what Mrs. Bienenmald says."

"Mrs. Bienenmald talks through her hat," Claire said airily. It was easier, now that she was twelve and five feet seven inches tall, to disregard their neighbor's pronouncements.

"She does? I never saw her do that. What kind of hat?"

"It's just an expression. It means she's full of beans."

"She is?" Dick smacked himself in the forehead and giggled. "Beans, beans, the musical fruit...."

"Not that kind of beans, silly. It just means she says a lot of things that are dumb."

"I'm gonna tell," Dick teased, obviously not meaning it.

"Go ahead." She smiled at him.

"Mrs. Bienenmald says making a pie is selfish. She says think of the poor starving children in Europe."

"It's Christmas. We're having pie. I'm sorry the children are starving, but there isn't anything I can do about it. I didn't start the stupid war."

"I know." Dick rested his face against his fists, frowning.

"Anyway, the kind I'm making is called 'Patriot's Pie.'" Claire showed him the recipe in the Woman's Day magazine. "See?"

Dick's face brightened. He leaned forward and started to read the list of ingredients. "I'm the best reader in third grade."

"I know you are. That's great." At least his reading was good. The rest of his grades this year had been pretty poor. Something was bothering Dick, but every time she asked he just said, "Nothing," and left the room.

As she measured the shortening and dropped it into the bowl, Claire rehearsed in her mind the menu for Christmas dinner. Chicken with stuffing, mashed potatoes, and canned tomatoes with a smidgen of hoarded butter and breadcrumbs. Poor Dad. He was going to have to kill one of the chickens. Raising chickens in the back yard meant they would always have meat and eggs, but Claire loathed gathering the eggs because the stupid chickens pooped on them and you had to wash off that sticky green stuff. Pulling out the feathers was no fun either, but Dad usually did that.

Dick began turning pages. "Don't lose my place," Claire warned.

"I'm keeping my finger on the right page," he protested. "Can we have pancakes for supper? With bacon and jelly?"

"That's a good idea. Pancakes will be easy. I already have the mix." What a long time had passed since they had had real maple syrup and enough butter to really make things delicious. At least the war had not come to New Jersey. Not yet, anyway. Things were terrible in Europe. On the radio she'd heard the announcer talk about the Battle of the Bulge. She wasn't sure what that was, but she knew that thousands of American soldiers had been killed already.

"'Mmm-my! Folks sho' goes fo' my dee-licious down south pan-cakes! Happify yo' pancake hungry family!' What does happify mean, Claire?"

"I don't think it's a real word, but I guess it's supposed to mean you make your family happy. It makes you happy when I make pancakes, doesn't it?"

"Yeah, but you don't say 'happify.' That's dumb." He turned back to the recipe page. "Aunt Jemima always wears a rag on her head. I know why. Do you?"

"Rosy the Riveter wears a kerchief on her head."

"Does she have cooties?"

"Of course not. It's so she won't get her hair caught in the ma-chinery where she does war work. Why would you think she has cooties?"

"Mrs. Bienenmald says colored people have cooties so they have to wear a rag on their heads to keep them from falling into the pan-cake batter." He made a face.

"Don't listen to her. She's crazy," Claire said. "Here. Why don't you help? You can grate the orange peel for me."

An hour later, she took the pie from the oven. Beautifully browned, it smelled so wonderful it was all she could do not to grab a spoon and eat the whole thing.

* * *

Claire sat in the rocking chair Dad had brought upstairs, holding a squirmy Stevie in her lap. Once again she was reading him "The

Little Engine That Could."

"Don't you want me to read something else? Little Toot? Peter Churchmouse?"

"No," Stevie said. "It's my best story. *I think I can, I think I can, I think I can, I knew I could, I knew I could.* Yea!" He clapped his pudgy hands together.

She hugged him, relishing his warmth. At three and a half, he was still cuddly, but he was no longer a baby. He had a mind of his own and the legs to take him there.

After finishing the story she read him "The Night Before Christmas."

"Is tomorrow really Christmas?"

"Don't you remember? We hung up your stocking? And decorated the tree? And put out graham crackers for Santa?"

"Because we don't have any cookies." Stevie yawned.

"Santa likes graham crackers, too." Claire lifted him off her lap and nudged him in the direction of the bathroom. He was sleeping through the night without a diaper, but she always made him go one more time.

"I'm not tired, Calaire," he protested as she picked him up and set him on the bed. He yawned again; his eyelids fluttered. "Can't I stay up until Dick goes to bed?"

"I have a job for you," she said. "You just lie here quietly and watch out the window for Santa and his reindeer. When you see them, call me and I'll come and we can tiptoe downstairs and watch him fill our stockings. Okay? Will you do that?"

Stevie's eyes widened. "O-kay. I promise." He knelt on his bed by the window peering up into the sky. "It's starting to snow. I hope he gets here before it's too snowy."

"He will." Claire kissed him and tucked him in. "Good night, Bunny Boy."

"Night, Calaire."

It was time to round up Dick, but he wasn't in his room or in any of the rooms upstairs. Claire smiled to herself as she went downstairs and passed the living room where Mother and Dad were talking in voices too soft for her to make out what they were saying. She was so glad they were happier these days, she didn't want to disturb them. Dick had to be somewhere nearby. He wouldn't go anywhere on Christmas Eve.

After searching the entire house, including the front porch and the basement, Claire was getting worried. As she passed through the kitchen, she saw that Dick's jacket wasn't hanging on the coat hook. Maybe he'd gone outside to watch for Santa. She slipped her coat on and went out the back door.

With a dusting of snow on the ground, finding Dick was easy. His footprints led to the chicken coop, behind the garage. She could see dim light coming through the crack under the door. What was he doing in there? Dick didn't even like chickens. She almost opened the door and then thought maybe she should give him some warning, in case he was eating smuggled food or reading something he shouldn't like horror comics. She knocked. The light went out. She knocked again. "Dick?"

"Go away. I'm not here."

"Then who am I talking to? Joe Clark Bar?"

She heard a snicker. "Joe Clark Bar got killed in the war."

Claire's heart lurched. Was that why Dick had been so upset all fall? "He did? That's terrible. When did that happen?"

"On Mom's birthday. His plane got shot down. It fell into the ocean and he drowneded."

Mom's birthday was December 7th. Dick had been upset for months. Something else was bothering him. "I'm sorry to hear about Joe. Can I come in?"

She heard him sigh. "Okay."

"Turn the flashlight back on so I can see."

"Okay."

The musty odor of chicken assailed Claire's nose. A couple of the hens made soft clucking noises, as if to complain about their sleep being disturbed. Dick had made a pile of clean straw to sit on. Claire sat beside him. His face looked sticky in the dim light.

"Did you take some pie while I was reading to Stevie?" she

asked.

"No."

"I smell something sweet."

"No, you don't."

She hugged him. "Never mind. It's okay. I felt like eating the whole pie all by myself."

"So did I, but I didn't." Sheepishly Dick reached behind him and pulled out a small can of condensed milk with a spoon stuck in it. "Are you gonna tell?"

So that's where the condensed milk had gone. "Tell who? Myself? I'm the cook."

"But you prob'ly need it for something."

"It's okay, Dick. We have enough food. Thanks for not eating the pie."

"You're welcome." He dipped the spoon into the can and offered it to Claire. Bits of straw clung to the sticky stuff. "Want some?"

"No, thanks. You finish it." She watched him lick it off the spoon, straw and all. "We'd better go in before Santa gets here."

"Santa's your parents. Everybody knows that."

"Well, then we'd better go to bed so they can fill our stockings and put out the presents."

Dick sighed. "Yeah."

"Dick?"

"What?"

"Why are you out here?"

He shrugged. "No reason."

"To eat the condensed milk?"

"No."

"Then what?"

"Nothing."

"I won't tell. I know something's been bothering you for a long time. Is it about school?"

"I told you. It's nothing." Dick stood up. "Let's go in."

Claire picked up the empty can and spoon and followed him out of the chicken coop. She shut the door tightly behind them. As she crossed the yard, she stopped to set the can on the back steps and reached for Dick's hand. "Come here for a minute." She pulled him into the front yard and looked across the street. The Goehners' house looked all blurry through the sifting snow. Of course, it hadn't been the Goehners' house since Stevie was a baby. A family named Headley lived there now. "I hope they're having a nice Christmas. I wish I knew where they went."

"They went to prison. That's what Mrs. Bienenmald said. She said they were spies and they got put in prison and killed. Even Carl got killed."

Claire's heart clenched. That couldn't be true. They had been such nice people. Carl had been her best friend. Second best. "How would she know that?"

"From the news. She says if you listen to the radio you know there's lots of German spies around here. They come and get them and put them in jail and tie a rag around their eyes and shoot them and their blood runs all over the ground and they get a hose and wash it away. And then they steal their shoes and throw their bodies into a big hole." He looked up at Claire, his eyes full of fear. "And then they put dirt on top of them, even if they're not dead yet."

"Who comes and gets them?"

Dick slapped some snow off his face. "The FBI."

"Oh, Dick. I don't think so." But she remembered the three men and the dark car from the summer of 1941 and wasn't so sure.

"Yeah, well, what if it happens to us? What if they take our house and our car and my toys and everything? What if they take us away like they did Carl?"

"We don't know what happened to Carl. Maybe the Goehners just went somewhere else."

"Because they knew the FBI was coming to get them?"

"I don't know. I wish you wouldn't listen to Mrs. Bienenmald. She doesn't know any more than we do. She makes stuff up just to be mean."

"Well, then, why do Mom and Dad talk at night all the time and

84

you can't hear what they're saying even if you tiptoe downstairs and listen as hard as you can? Maybe Dad's a spy. He works for the government and he works on secret stuff." Dick lowered his voice and whispered. "Radar. Maybe he's helping the Germans. Maybe Mom is just pretending to be sick."

"Why would she do that?"

"So she could call up the Germans on the telephone and tell them stuff. You can't hear because you're always taking care of Stephen and cooking and washing the dishes and I'm in bed and I can't even hear what they're saying even if I'm quiet as a mouse. How would you like it if they shoot us and steal our shoes and throw *us* in a hole and put dirt on our heads when we're not even dead yet?"

"I won't let them, Dick." At last she knew what had been tormenting him for months. She put a hand on his shoulder. "Let's go inside where it's warm. You can read 'The Night Before Christmas' to Mother and Dad, show them what a good reader you are. Come on."

Dick put his head down and mumbled, "Okay."

After he went to bed she would have a talk with Mother and Dad. Maybe Mother would never take over the cooking and laundry again, but from now on she and Dad were going to keep the boys away from Mrs. Bienenmald *and* they were going to spend time with Dick in the evening instead of letting him be scared half to death. *Telling* Dick they weren't spies wouldn't be enough. Mother and Dad would have to *show* him and Claire was going to make sure they did.

Chapter
13

Phoebe's turning into quite a cook. Earlier this week she and I wrestled my mother's old rocker down from the attic and set it in the kitchen where I can supervise the food preparation and work on the burgundy scarf I'm knitting for her. I send prayers of thanks to the Universe, and Sean, the Turd (I can't believe I am thinking such a vile word!), for making it possible for her to be here with me. I feel so blessed.

A mixture of red wine and red wine vinegar is heating on the stove, filling the kitchen with a tang that is almost narcotic. Phoebe has sliced an onion and placed it along with bay leaves, crushed peppercorns, and juniper berries on top of the beautiful rump roast we purchased yesterday. It's Friday evening. We'll have the sauerbraten on Sunday evening. If we can wait that long!

Once she has poured the hot vinegar/wine mixture over the meat into the bowl and placed a plate over it, she sits down at the table. Earlier that afternoon, from a box of my mother's things in the attic, she unearthed a copy of Woman's Day, March 1942. We decided to look at it together.

The girl on the cover has a Shirley Temple hairstyle with a simple bow at the top of her head. She has her arm around a fluffy white dog with perky ears and bright eyes. The girl would be in her sixties now, if she's alive. It tugs at my heart to think that dear little dog is so long gone. Silly of me, but there you are. I'm a pushover when it comes to dogs. Ringo is lying under the table, his muzzle resting on my feet.

The pages are brown-edged and tattered. We turn the pages with care, coming upon a column of letters from readers. Phoebe reads part of one aloud.

A year ago I was frantic with war news and worries. Now I am not. The secret is work. Help win this war. Every red-blooded American woman and girl can have a part and should, for the sake of the soldier boys. Get interested, give an afternoon or two a week to the Red Cross, help them roll bandages, help them knit, help them sew, take a First Aid course, a home nursing course, work with the home nutrition group on food conservation.

She sighs. "Soldier boys. That's so sad."

"War is sad. Soldier girls is sad, too."

She nods and reads on.

Above all, keep yourself cool. Do not listen to more than one news broadcast each day."

"Good advice." I remember that horrible day--9/11. I stood in my kitchen staring at the five-inch black and white TV, transfixed for hours, until Ringo belted me with his head and looked toward the door. That walk saved my sanity, though I wept the whole time.

We turn more pages. Phoebe shrieks. "Look at that furniture. Did anyone seriously think that was pretty?"

The love seat she's looking at was described as having been bought second-hand for $5.00, and covered with black chintz with enormous appliqued pink chrysanthemums. Total cost $12.73. It is a horror.

"They should have saved their money."

The women's fashions are even more ghastly and look only faintly familiar. Had Mom worn clothes like that? I can't remember how she dressed, except for the bathrobes. The prices are unbelievable. Vogue pattern, $.35, fabric $2.59, notions $.60. What really catches the eye is the model standing humbly next to a desk at which a stuffy-looking man in suit and tie sits, eyeing some papers with the expression of someone who has stepped in something nasty left by the family dog.

"I'm glad those days are past. The one good thing that came out of the war was making it easier for women to hold jobs. Of course, when the 'boys' came back from the war the women were fired and the magazines tried to sell them a bill of goods about 'togetherness,' but the horse was out of the barn. Women learned that having a paying job gave them freedom. They didn't have to beg for money from their husbands, or seduce them into sharing some of 'his' money."

"Oh, yuck, Gran," Phoebe said, aghast. "That's like...prostitution."

"No one would have dared call it that, but that was what many mothers told their daughters they'd have to do, or so I heard later from older friends." I find I have dropped a stitch and have to unknit an entire row to pick it up.

"Chattel," she mutters.

"Working and earning money changed the balance of power."

"Men still have more power," Phoebe grumbles.

"Only as much as you give them."

"Oh, come on. They have power because...you care about them."

"A man with self-respect would know better and a man who cared about you wouldn't treat you like that." Link had been that kind of man. How I miss him every minute of every day. How could that dear soul be gone? As for Sean, what had he done to my Phoebe?

Phoebe pulls me away from my heartache, pointing to an ad for Aunt Jemima pancake mix. A smiling brown skinned woman wearing a pink bandana grins out from the page. "Mmm-my! Folks sho' goes fo' my dee-licious Down South pancakes! Happify yo' pancake hungry family!"

I remember how disgusted Dick was when he read "happify" so many years ago from this same magazine.

"Oh, for the good ol' days." Phoebe closes the magazine. "That's enough nostalgia for one day."

"Nostalgia is not so much about things as remembering when you felt all new yourself and everything was magical. Everything was spring. Even thinking about that nasty, oh, maybe I should be kind and say misguided neighbor of ours, brings back those funny/ sad/poignant feelings. Back when my brother Dick was only five and had an imaginary playmate, Joe Clark Bar, and your great uncle Stephen was a newborn, I despised that woman. In retrospect she couldn't have been very bright. No excuse, of course. I'm convinced she brought a lot of misery to my friend Carl and his family. But those memories are all tied with the gorgeous blue hydrangeas that grew in her yard, and the robins that nested in the mulberry tree in our yard. To this day when I hear a robin, I am eight years old and living on Atlantic Lane."

Phoebe's eyes light up. "We should go there sometime. You could show me your old house and where Carl lived. You said you wanted to go see Great Grandma. I'll go with you. It'll be fun. We'll go to the shore and have a fish dinner. Maybe we can find where that Japanese guy lived. American Japanese guy, that is."

I take her face in my hands and kiss her cheek. "You know, I've been dreading that drive, but if we go together, it would be great. We'll go for Mother's birthday. I'll make her a cake like the one I made in 1941. We didn't know it was Pearl Harbor Day until later, and she refused to eat anything at all."

Another pang hits my heart as I wish I could see my father as he was that day, so kindly in his treatment of Mr. Nishida. So dear and funny, with enough love to make up for the gaps left by Mother's depression.

I stand up. "You're right. Enough with the nostalgia already. Let's fire up the dog and go for a walk. We can plan our trip."

"I'll get your sweater," Phoebe says.

Chapter 14

Phoebe's due in for lunch any time now. Her eleven o'clock usually runs a little late. I've assured her I was quite fine with her eating on campus with friends, but she insists she likes coming home. She actually does call it "home," which touches me more than I care to admit.

"You'll probably have moved by next year," she pointed out the other evening, "and I don't want to miss out on any grandmother time, or being in this house. Promise me you'll sell it to somebody who deserves it."

There's a pot of chicken soup on the stove and cornbread cooling on a trivet, so I can put in a few more minutes in this attic. It's still fairly warm for late September. Good thing. We have a lot of clearing out to do before it gets too cold to work up here.

I move a few boxes and come upon Link's trunk from college. I'm not sure I can bear to open it and find the remnants of that boy/man he was when I first knew him. If only I could get that precious time back, even just for a day. Did I know then how precious? I'd like to think I did.

I continue to sit there too long, waffling, until I hear Phoebe's bug drive in. Moments later, she calls up from the kitchen, "Gran?"

"Up here, sweetie."

She is upstairs in moments, her face ruddy with the exertion of running up two sets of stairs. She is smiling.

"Something good?" I ask.

"I aced my astronomy test. You may touch me."

"Gosh. Am I worthy?" I reach to press a finger against her arm.

She blows a raspberry and sits on a box near me. She points to the trunk. "Grandpa's from long ago." She looks sad. "Must be hard. I can't imagine it."

"And I can't begin to tell you."

"Let me do it." She opens the trunk. On top is a faded green t-shirt with the words, "Camp Chaffee, Staff," across the front. "What's this?"

"Camp Chaffee is where I met your grandfather."

"Love at first sight?"

"Not quite. I was pretty interested in the lifeguard. Yes, I know. A cliché, but he *was* cute." I smile into the past. "That didn't last long. Your grandpa had something special, something I didn't see at first glance, but once I did, the die was cast."

"Tell me, Gran," she says with a sigh. "I could stand to hear a love story with a happy ending, unlike mine."

"Oh, Honey, I know that hurts, but the right one will come along, when you least expect it. Someone who deserves you." I push to my feet, trying not to look like an old lady with aches and pains. "Let's go down for lunch. You have a two o'clock and I have a dentist appointment at three."

I put out blue and yellow flowered placemats and yellow plates and bowls. Phoebe pours herself a glass of milk. I have Earl Grey tea.

Phoebe sniffs the soup and smiles. "Okay, Gran. Story time."

I break my square of cornbread and butter one of the halves. "I was a delegate to Camp Chaffee, a camp attended by kids from all over the world where we discussed international relations and world peace. And after all these years we still don't have it. I was pushing eighteen, about to start college, and full of idealism.

"It was a Saturday night in August, on the warm side for Vermont. The camp dining hall was packed and rocking with the thunder of young male voices and the counterpoint of girls' higher pitched tones. Moths fluttered frantically around the light bulbs. I waited by the main door until the food line was short, even though that meant pickings would be slim. I was suffering from too much togetherness, a concept of great currency in the postwar years.

"I remember stealing a look at the staff table to see if John Ball, camp lifeguard, was among them. We called boys with builds like his 'dreamy' in those days. You'd probably say 'hunk' now. 'Dreamy' and 'hunk.' What a lot those terms say about the changes in society in fifty years! Class leaders were almost always boys. We called them BMOCs — Big Men on Campus, but the boys at Camp Chaffee were more the types to major in poli sci and belong to the history club. Geeks. Cool geeks, though neither of those slang words was current back then."

"So what about this John?" Phoebe tastes her soup. "Yum. Is there lemon in it?"

"Well, of course. Let's see. John was a senior at Penn State and on the swim team. After discussion groups, I hung out on the dock half the afternoon, risking sunburn in my blue and white strapless bathing suit, hoping he'd notice me, watching him go through his paces, muscles rippling as he swam from the dock to the float and back, over and over. Be still, my heart!" I pat myself on the chest and bat my eyelashes. Phoebe laughs.

"I paid for it. My shoulders were a fiery red and burning hot under my camp shirt. I didn't dare think what the backs of my legs looked like, but I knew they'd keep me awake that night and peel by the end of the week, which they did.

"I grabbed a tray, a chipped plate, and a couple pieces of the battered silverware. There were still some chunks of a meatloafish kind of stuff, lots of lukewarm butter beans, a spoonful of mashed potatoes, and plenty of rolls and butter. I took my tray out to the porch where it was cooler and quieter. I set the tray on the railing and looked out at the lake. I remember it so clearly. The water, almost perfectly smooth but for an occasional ripple, was bathed in pink and gold from the sun filtering through the pines on the hillside. Something, a bat maybe, flew by. Bugs of some sort buzzed in the weeds. A pair of frogs conducted a frenzied colloquy down by the dock."

Phoebe hoots with laughter. "Only you, Grandmother, would use 'frenzied colloquy' in a conversation."

"Hush, Phoeb. That's what it was. I just want you to get the picture," I tell her. "Moving right along...a couple of ducks fussed their way along the shoreline. Out in the middle of the lake a pair of people paddled a canoe, unaware no doubt of how well voices carry over water.

"The meatloaf was pretty bad. I think I can still remember how it smelled. I pushed it aside and ate a few beans and a bite of mashed potatoes. I set the tray on the floor and put my elbows on the railing, looking for the first star. Waiting for something. Waiting for John, maybe. Waiting for my 'life' to start. Missing your Great Uncle Steve terribly. For heaven's sake, he was nine years old by then, Mom was doing fairly okay, he didn't need me, but the separation was a physical as well as emotional pain.

"Someone rang a cowbell inside the dining hall, enough times to make me want to throttle whoever it was. Raucous singing broke out. Some sort of talent show was planned for later that evening.

"Despite the volume of sound I could hear footsteps approaching me. I waited, hands clutching the railing, forcing myself not to turn around. I imagined John putting his hands on my shoulders, well, not my poor shoulders. 'Hi, gorgeous,' he'd say. 'Want to go down to the dock and watch the submarine races?'

"Submarine races? In a lake? Are you kidding me, Grandmother?"

"That was slang for going off somewhere and smooching. Of course, I would have said no, but I might have agreed to go for a walk.

"'Noisy, isn't it?' The voice was soft and kind of baritonish, but without John's telltale Philadelphia twang.

"Disappointed, I turned to see who it was. Link Hanneman, bearded, gnarly, with a goofy crusher hat perched high on his head. He smiled tentatively. He's shy, I thought, surprised, because he seemed so confident when he led discussions after workshops. I knew he was a grad student at Columbia, five or six years older than I.

"When I just nodded, he went on to say, 'You in the talent show?'

"I shrugged and rolled my eyes, dippy girl style. 'I don't exactly have any talent you could put on stage.'

"'I bet you do, but some of us, like me, have to be appreciators.' He joined me at the railing, gesturing toward the lake. 'Pretty nice show.'

"Yeah," I said with great eloquence. We stood there watching the people in the canoe put down their paddles and attempt to get together in the middle, climbing carefully over the struts. Their love talk came over the water, loud and clear. We were both a little embarrassed--it was 1950, remember--so we turned away from the lake and ended up looking at each other."

"Sigh," Phoebe says, grinning at me.

"Show some respect for your elders," I mock scold.

"I'm sorry, I'm sorry. Keep going, with lots of detail."

I take a sip of tea. "A blare of trumpet music exploded from the dining hall, followed by cheers and a drum roll. More laughter.

"'It's quieter down by the dock.' He invited me with a head gesture.

"Just then, the female of the canoe people let out a bloodcurdling shriek and the boat turned over.

"Link laughed. 'Well, not so quiet. Maybe they need help. Come on.' He started down the steps, running toward the dock.

"'Help,' the girl screamed. 'I can't swim.'

"'Hang onto the canoe,' he yelled. 'We'll be right there.'

"'If I hadn't followed him, you probably wouldn't be here to-day."

"Many thanks to those people, I guess." Phoebe takes a bite of cornbread. "Continue."

"'So, follow him I did. I got in the rowboat and we went out on the lake. Your grandfather was kind of skinny, but he was wiry and a strong rower. We reached the capsized couple in no time. Link hauled the girl up out of the water and the boy pulled himself in, dripping all over the bottom of the boat. Between the two males,

94

they managed to dump the water out of the canoe and tie it to the back of the rowboat. In the meanwhile, the paddles had floated dangerously close to the dam, so we went to get them and pulled the canoe to shore since neither of the pair wanted to get back in.

"Link helped lug the canoe to dry ground while I held onto the dock from the rowboat. The lovebirds were soaked and sneezing, but they thanked us profusely, laughing now that they were safe, and headed for their respective cabins to get dry clothes.

"While we were rescuing people the moon came up, a new moon, a silver sliver in the dark sky that laid a rippled mirror image on the water. By then the bugs had settled down for the night. The ducks went somewhere. We sat on the end of the dock, me dangling my feet, carefully because of my sunburn, Link sitting cross-legged and leaning against a post."

Phoebe puts down her soup spoon. "We are getting to the good part soon, aren't we?"

I laugh. "Don't expect anything racy from me, Toots."

She sticks out her lower lip, but her eyes are full of mirth. How I love this child/woman.

"'You're a senior,' he said. 'What're you doing next year?'

"'Gettysburg. My dad thinks I need to get far away from home.'

"'And you don't?' He tilted his head and looked at me quizzically. 'Most kids can't wait to get away.'

"'It's kind of a strange situation. On the one hand, I'm looking forward to it, on the other hand, it's just so far and I worry.'

"'About?'

"'My little brother. I've practically raised him. My mother was sick for the first four years of his life and I took care of him. Mom's better now, but Stevie and I are still close. He's nine.'

"'You must have been pretty young to be taking care of a baby. How'd you know what to do?'

"'You learn fast when you have to.' I thought about Liesl Goehner, but didn't want to get into all of that.

"'What kind of sick?'

"In those days no one talked about depression, but I felt I could say anything to this guy.

"'It started out to be what they called baby blues and then it was the war and Mom's family in England, and, I don't know. She just slept all the time, when she wasn't crying. She wasn't up to taking care of Stephen. She was a great mother with me and my brother Dick.' I guess I must have sighed. 'If I could just hear Stevie's voice, so I'd know he was okay. It's almost like he's my kid instead of my brother.'

"'There's no phone here, except the one locked in the infirmary and it's only for emergencies.'

"'I know.' There was still another week to go before camp ended.

"'I'm pretty close with my brother, only he's a lot older than I am,' Link said after a long pause that surprisingly wasn't at all uncomfortable. 'I miss him if I don't see him at least once a month, and talk once a week. I didn't see him for two years during the war. I was fifteen and sixteen while he was gone.'

"'I hate war,' I said. 'Sometimes I think the people who make guns and tanks started the whole thing, just to make money.'

"'Spoken like a true Camp Chaffee-ite.' He took off his hat and scratched his head. 'Kit wasn't in the service. He was in prison.'

"People these days would have a hard time understanding the shock and power of the word 'prison' back then, the shame and fear that word evoked. I remember pulling slightly away from him, thinking, Good Lord. What did his brother do? Rob a bank? Kill somebody?

"Link said, 'He went to prison for being a Conscientious Objector. He believed killing was wrong. Still does, and so do I. He could have gone to a work camp and at least been outside, but because he was studying to be a minister, they sent him to a Federal prison where he served as chaplain. We're all really proud of him. It must have been unbelievably hard. He wrote a letter home every week. I still have them.'

"'Prison must be horrible, but war's a whole lot worse. One of the neighbor's boys came back without his legs. My cousin died in the Pacific. He was only sixteen. He lied about his age and nobody caught it, or they just took him anyway.' *And Carl disappeared.*

"'Human beings have a long way to go on the evolutionary scale.' He put his hat back on, tugged it in place, whatever that was."

Phoebe laughs. "I remember Grandpa's hats."

"I said to him, 'I thought only Quakers could be Conscientious Objectors, but Quakers don't have ministers, do they?'

"'I'm not sure,' he admitted. 'We're Unitarians. We have a long history of opposing war, too.'

"'I never even *heard* of Unitarians.'

"'There aren't that many of us,' he said with a rueful shrug.

"I smiled at him. 'If they're against war, I think I'd like to be one.'

"He smiled back at me. He was actually a lot cuter than I had first thought. Nothing could have prepared me for what he said next.

"'So, here's a thought. Marry me. After you get out of school, I mean. Or after camp's over. Tomorrow?'

"You're kidding," Phoebe croaks, delight in her eyes.

"Nope. That's what he said."

"And you said...?"

"'What?' My mouth must have hung open halfway to my chest.

"'Well, think about it. The idea has definite merit in my opinion.'

"'You're totally crazy.' I shook my head, but I had to laugh. Turned out he wasn't all that shy. 'That was about as romantic as my first marriage proposal.'

"'I could get down on one knee.'

"'Don't you dare,' I whispered.

"'Okay, I won't.' He grabbed my left hand and inspected the third finger. 'Tell me you're not engaged.'

"'Well, I still have the ring, but I don't know what happened to him.'

"That's the ring I found in the dresser," Phoebe says, excited.

"Carl's grandmother's ring."

"That's the one."

"Then what?"

"Link said, 'Maybe he died of a broken heart.' He took off his hat and placed it over his sternum. 'La Belle Dame Sans Merci.'

"His accent was quite good, but with a hint of New York City. I had taken four years of French in high school, so I responded in kind. 'J'avais huit ans, idiot.'

"The look on his face made me worry he was going to propose again, or maybe try to kiss me, so I hurried on to explain about what had happened to Carl and his parents. 'Maybe he gave me the ring so the FBI wouldn't take it. There was nothing romantic about our friendship.'

"'Sounds like he knew something was up.'

"'Probably. He was only nine, the same as Stevie is now, but way more mature. His mother was wonderful. I would never have gotten through that summer without her help.'

"'Do you think they were Nazi sympathizers?'

"I gave him a dirty look. 'Absolutely not. They were lovely people. Carl was my best friend.'

"'You never found out anything about what happened?'

"'I tried. I wrote to President Roosevelt, twice, to ask if he knew where they were. I finally got an answer, a form letter, thanking me for my interest in the democratic process. Dear fill in the blank Claire.'

"'Signed by him at least?'

"'They must have made a rubber stamp that looked like his signature. The signature was sort of faded at one end, as if they hadn't inked it enough. Well, he was busy and I was just a little girl of no importance.'

"Just then the curfew gong rang. Eleven o'clock already. I jumped up and then yelped. 'My sunburn.'

"'You did spend quite a lot of time on dock duty today,' Link teased.

"I was embarrassed that he'd noticed.

98

"He stood up. 'If I promise not to propose tomorrow, I'm taking the truck into town to pick up some supplies. You could go along. There's a pay phone in the hotel. You could call your family and, if you really are interested, there's a Unitarian fellowship we could check out. If not, there's a great place to get pancakes. They serve them with real Vermont butter and maple syrup.'

"I scarcely hesitated. 'Could we possibly do both?'

"Your grandpa threw his hat in the air. It sailed into the water. 'Yes,' he shouted. 'We can do both.' And then he jumped into the lake with all his clothes on."

Chapter
15

I am running down dark, rain-drenched streets. Somehow I know it is well past midnight. I am in Paris, pursued by Nazis, dozens of them. I hear their jackboots clatter on the cobblestones. Their voices are harsh. I dart into an alley and hide behind a wooden cart, but they know where I am and converge on the alley, pointing their big guns in my direction.

I cry out and awake in a sweat. It has been well over a year since I had this dream. Link was still alive the last time and he reached for me then. "Bad dream?"

"The Nazi dream." I didn't have to explain further.

Why have I had these nightmares all my life? My only experience of direct warfare was through the newsreels and the newspaper. Why would I think Nazis were after *me*? Was it something to do with Carl's disappearance? Had my child's eye view of the world thought someone would come to take us, too? Could it have been the Nazis who took Carl and his family, spiriting them away from capture by U.S. agents? Or was it the U.S. agents? Had Mr. Goehner in fact been a spy? Or was he an ordinary man trying to do his job and take care of his family?

He had been kindly but vague toward us kids, never one to play with us like my father did. I've read in history books that Nazi officers could send thousands to a death camp in the day and return home to wife and children in the evening, to enjoy a fine meal, good wine, and listen to classical music on the radio. Had the Goehners gone to Germany? If so, had Carl stayed there? That would explain why he never looked for me. Of course, we moved from Atlantic Lane in the fall of 1945, just six months after the

U.S. declared victory in Europe. He would have had difficulty finding us. Mrs. Bienenmald, the witch, would never have given our forwarding address to him.

Ringo parks his long nose on the bedcovers. Come on, Claire, he seems to say. Get up, take a shower, and let's have breakfast.

* * *

I can't believe Hallowe'en is just around the corner. Nor can I believe how much Phoebe and I have accomplished in the two months she's been here. Good thing because the weather has turned cold. Even with a heavy sweater, I am shivering in the frigid air in the attic. The first snow of the season fell this morning. A mere dusting today, but by January the white stuff will be piled ten feet deep along the county road. We'll finish the last few boxes when spring returns. There's plenty to do in the rest of the house.

The last thing I take downstairs is a boot box marked "photos." I carry it to the kitchen and place it on the table. Phoebe has a lunchtime study session with some classmates from her history class, so I make a peanut butter and cheese sandwich and a cup of tea for my lunch, planning to look through the jumble of photographs. Neither Link nor I was the type to put them in scrapbooks. They're still in the envelopes we got back from the photo shop.

As I eat, I think how much I love my kitchen. I love this whole house, with its nooks and crannies, its walk-in pantry, the fireplaces, the views. How will I ever find a place to live I love as much? Do I care if I love it? Without the people, the history of loving and working, and even fighting, the place will be walls and roof, with some familiar furniture and most of our books. At least, in another place, I won't keep expecting to see Link at his desk, working on a paper, or devising a test; won't think he's just outside, pruning the rhododendron, or tossing a stick for the dog to retrieve. And have my heart broken all over again.

Ringo gets up from his bed by the back door, slinks under the table, and lies down, his warm paws on my feet. "Good boy," I tell him. I even slip him a bit of my sandwich. He scarfs it down and grunts with pleasure.

Pawing through the envelopes, I look for one dated October 1985. Link had been invited to give a paper at a symposium in Munich that summer. We decided a trip to France and Germany would be our vacation that year, with a visit to Paris, then on to the symposium. We could take side trips as time allowed. I wasn't at all sure I wanted to go to Germany, but Link was committed.

At last I find the right envelope and then freeze. I want to look at the pictures and I don't. Grief wells up and I put the packet aside for later. I almost envy my friend Charlotte who, weeping after her husband's funeral last spring, whispered to me that she was crying, not because Leo was dead, but because she was finally free. At least she doesn't ache with loss every day. But then, her entire life with Leo was one long grief. I am better off, I know, not that it helps all that much. I am so grateful that Phoebe is here.

She's doing an oral history project for her history class. She is fascinated by the story of the disappearance of my young friend, Carl. When she gets back from school I'll tell her about looking for his relatives in Germany.

The day is perfect for a fire in the den fireplace. I build one and then settle on the couch with a crocheted afghan across my legs, the packet of photographs on my lap. I was never one for having my picture taken in front of this or that castle, or ruin, or what have you, but when we visited Rottweil, a young German woman asked us in perfect English if we would like her to take our picture. Of course we said yes since she was so friendly and eager. How young we look, though I was in my early fifties and Link fifty-nine. My arm is linked through his as we pose on a side street in front of a driving school. A plaque on the wall says that the building housed a synagogue, until 1938. I remember that I shuddered and, after the young woman had gone on her way, asked why we were there. "To find your friend's family," Link reminded me with utmost kindness.

* * *

At a small restaurant in Munich we ordered the onion pie and the new wine, local fall specialties. The pie was almost sweet and had a consistency not unlike stewed rhubarb. I couldn't decide if I liked it. The wine, too, was sweet, and more like fruit juice than an alcoholic beverage. Neither Link nor I could eat or drink much, nor did we have much to say. Our visit to Dachau was a third party at the table, a starving, gaunt, tortured wraith gazing at the abundance on our plates.

So cold it was that October day we visited the camp, with the rain pouring endlessly from the sky, the tears running endlessly down my face. All but one of the barracks that housed the prisoners was gone, with only the outlines on the ground to show where they had been. *Arbeit Macht Frei.* Work Makes Free. Shivery. The ovens, the memorials. All too much. The very ground seemed drenched with evil.

"Why did we go there?" I asked.

Link set down his fork and reached for my hand. "Because deep down we hoped it never happened." He planted a kiss in my palm. "That the pictures were somehow faked."

"Well, I believe it now and I want to go home."

"Not yet," he said with a wry smile. "I haven't given my paper and you haven't found your friend's relatives."

"Do you realize it's been thirty-five years since Camp Chaffee? Remember how we talked about world peace? About understanding other points of view? About respecting the truths of other religions? About caring for one another? Things are worse than ever in the world, not better." I thought I had wept myself dry, but more tears welled up.

Link signaled to the waiter.

"Is something wrong, sir?" he asked.

Link nodded. "We visited the camp today."

The waiter, far too young to remember the war, produced a check. "Many people have that reaction. I am sorry that you could not enjoy your meal. We are well known for our onion pie."

Sunshine filtered down through thinning clouds. The smell of apples filled the chilly air. Arm in arm we walked the streets of

Munich. In the morning we would look for Mrs. Goehner's relatives.

* * *

Phoebe changes the tape on the little recording machine she has previously set on the coffee table. The crackle of the fire is comforting. "So then what?"

"I had the address of Mrs. Goehner's relative, a cousin apparently. At the corner of the street where this person lived was a building with a sign 'Kindergarten' on the front. Children were laughing and playing in the yard, like children anywhere. After Dachau, it was such a disconnect for me."

Phoebe looks up at me. Her skin is so smooth, so young, such a lovely shade of coffee and cream, I have to touch her cheek with my mottled, crooked fingers. "If they made Liberty Cabbage out of sauerkraut," she says, "you'd think they would have stopped calling that grade 'kindergarten.'"

"I guess we had used the word so long it probably seemed American. Sort of like hummus and pita bread do now."

Phoebe mock scolds me with a shake of her forefinger. "But we digress, Grandmother. I assume you didn't find the cousin."

I shake my head. "The woman who answered the door-—a lean, faded blonde with bulging blue eyes--told us she had lived in that house for more than twenty years and knew no one with the last name of Ledergerber who had lived there in the past. 'I am sorry,' she apologized. 'My mother might have known those people, but she died fifteen years ago.'

"'I hoped somehow to learn the fate of my friend from childhood,' I told her. 'Sorry to have bothered you.'

"'It is no problem.' She gave me a tight smile. 'So many people were lost. For no good reason.'

"Power," Phoebe says grimly. "It's all about power. Wouldn't you love to know what went through Hitler's head just before he killed himself? 'Golly, gee willikers, I really messed up, didn't I?'"

"I suspect it was more like '*scheiss*!' But we'll never know, just like I'll never know what happened to Carl."

"The difference is you care about what happened to Carl."
Phoebe switches off the machine. "Thanks, Gran. I think I have
all I need for my project."

It's time for her to head back to campus and for me to put on
something more presentable for my trip to the dentist.

As I head to town I find myself back in Marlsburg where for
some reason it is always summer and every airplane that flies overhead might be a bomber.

Chapter 16

O ver breakfast on the twentieth of December Phoebe and I decide the time has come to buy a Christmas tree. She is amenable, but wistful this morning. Sean (the creep) called last night, after four months of silence. They talked long after Ringo and I retired. I didn't let myself fall asleep until after I heard her slow tread on the stair. I congratulate myself for not bounding out of bed to check on her state of mind.

It's hard not having that special someone at the holidays to buy for, to plan a surprise for, to buy a tree with. How well I know. Giving in to a voice from the past might be tempting, if ill advised.

The wintry morning invites us to partake of the festive atmosphere provided by the Town Council and most of Lyndon's shopkeepers. The air is crisp and pure, if damp. The "vintage" street lamps are tastefully swagged with greenery and red bows. Holiday music blares from temporarily installed speakers. On the corner in front of the historical museum, Harry Milner, mayor of our village, is roasting sugarcoated nuts in a copper pan, as he has done every year since 1978. They smell "most sentimental."

"No calories at Christmas, ladies," he promises, smiling from under a Santa hat.

We buy a bag to share and stroll past the shops, pausing from time to time to admire a display. We've already shipped packages to faraway family, but I haven't bought anything for Phoebe, nor has she for me. She claims she'll be happy with world peace and a hand knit scarf.

"The scarf I can do." As for me, I don't want or need anything but the one thing I can't have.

We pass Betty's Kitchen, a cafe Link and I often frequented on Saturdays, known for its soups, homemade bread, and excellent pie. We'll have lunch here later and I'll try to assess how much damage Sean (the creep) has inflicted. I link arms with Phoebe and tell her how glad I am she's here.

"Me, too, Gran," she says, with a heartfelt sigh. "Me, too."

The tree lot is at the end of the main drag, where Hellebore Way meets Pipsissewa Place. Whoever selected the names for the streets and roads of Lyndon must have picked them out of a book called "Flowers of New England with Names Having Three Syllables or More." The identity of the namer of streets has been lost in the mists of time. I like to imagine it was the wife of some long ago mayor, who would have preferred to run for office herself, but had to be contented with leaving an imprint of unconventional street names on the town.

The fence around the tree lot bears hand-lettered signs offering "Christmas Trees," "Hanukkah Bushes," "Solstice Shrubs." Hanukkah is crossed out, that holiday period having just passed. A Christmas song, sung by those damnable chipmunks, blares from a speaker.

A tall young man with dark hair and astonishingly blue eyes stands in front of the heated sales shack, pounding a fist into his other hand. He is wearing a blue ski cap and a Lyndon College warm-up jacket. "Help you, ladies?" He says "ladies," but he is looking only at Phoebe with gratifying interest. *Oh, good. Sean-is, begone-is!*

"Solstice or Christmas?" He grins at her. "Or both, just to be on the safe side?"

Phoebe turns back to look at me. "Both?" She knows I won't put up a Christmas tree until Christmas Eve day, but a solstice shrub will have to go up today or tomorrow.

"You sneak," I tease, but I don't really care. I'm just glad that a good-looking young man is paying her some attention. I hang back and pretend to weigh the merits of wreath versus spray.

I hear the young man giving the sales pitch about longer-lasting versus good-smelling trees. "Both. It has to last until Epiphany," I call after them. For a moment I am standing on the porch of Camp Chaffee while another young man asks if I'd like to go down by the dock where it's cooler. I think back to when Nate's baseball coach used to tell the kids when they got hurt to "walk through the pain." Easier said than done.

"Claire Hanneman. How *are* you?"

It is Wendy Morrow. She and Gene Warren, the man she calls her "partner," are co-ministers of the Lyndon Unitarian Church. She is a lanky redhead with a boatload of freckles and the warmest smile ever. She has called several times to ask after me since Link died, but never pushed me to come back to church. She always says she knows I'll do that when I'm ready.

"I'm doing well, Wendy. My granddaughter's spending the year with me while I clear out my house. We've come for a tree."

A slight frown forms between her eyebrows. "I guess I knew you'd want to move on, but I'll miss you." She gives me a good solid hug that feels so good I vow to do more hugging in the future.

"Plans?" she asks.

I shrug. "New Jersey. Near my mother. I'm hoping that the Universe will step in with some grand and glorious idea when I'm ready."

She describes an arc above her head with a gloved hand. "In letters of gold across the firmament." She turns as Phoebe approaches. "That's the granddaughter?"

I nod, proud as can be. "Phoebe." I make quick introductions.

The young man is shouldering an enormous balsam as easily as if it were a baseball bat.

Phoebe's cheeks are kissed by cold. She looks happy. "What do you think, Grandmother?"

I sniff the tree. "Wonderful, but...."

"It's perfect," she protests. "One third off, too."

"And we are going to get that behemoth home...how?"

"Oh, yeah. We brought the Bug." She shrugs and looks up at the nice young man. "We'll have to get the other car, Brad. You'll hold it for us, won't you?"

"He will if I pay him for it." I smile at the young man and he smiles back.

"I'd be glad to, ma'am." Dark eyelashes as thick as a garage broom frame those incredible blue eyes. He has good manners, too. Nice change from el creepo. "I can drop it off on my way home," he offers, eager as a puppy. "I've got a pickup. It's on the way. No trouble."

Evidently they've been discussing more than trees if he knows where we live. "If you're sure, I won't say no. I'll even let you carry it into the house." We all chuckle. Thank goodness for the healing power of humor.

Wendy Morrow pats my arm. "Nice meeting you, Phoebe. I'll call you, Claire," and off she goes.

I pay for the tree and Phoebe and I amble toward the restaurant. Hot soup and homemade bread sound awfully good and, with the young man coming later, Phoebe may be more willing to talk about that phone call.

The soup of the day is a dense chicken vegetable; the breads are German rye and a Tuscan white, both still warm from the oven. We dig in and for a few minutes curtail our conversational salvos to "Yum," and "Sublime."

As we slow down, Phoebe reaches across the table and takes hold of my hand. "Are you going to be all right, Grandmother? I mean, I know how horrible I felt after Sean dumped me, but that was just a one-year thing. After fifty years, it must be unbearable."

"At times."

"I guess if you thought you'd meet Grandpa again on the streets of gold someday, it would help."

"I've never understood the streets-of-gold thing. What would we do with gold in heaven? My heaven wouldn't be paved. There would be soft green grass, trees, birds, sunshine, rain, music, all the blackberries you could eat, all the books ever written, and a way to connect with all the people and animals you've ever loved." Carl comes to mind. Funny that I still think of him after so many years.

He'd be an old man now, if he's even alive.

"On the other hand," I continue, "heaven, if there is such a thing, might be something far more glorious than anything we mere mortals can imagine. It would be lovely to think Grandpa and I would be together again, somewhere, somehow, even as disembodied souls." I remember the line from Rilke that Link read at our wedding. "'The love which consists in this, that two solitudes protect and limit and greet each other.'" I start to feel sad and struggle with it. "I think probably all there is left of Grandpa is my memories."

"All of ours, too, Gran."

"More soup, Claire, and Claire's beautiful granddaughter?" Betty Frick, the roly-poly proprietress, has approached with a tureen. "There's pie if you're souped out. Pecan, pumpkin, mince." She turns toward the kitchen as if she can see through the wall. "Apple with homemade cinnamon ice cream?"

Phoebe's eyes light up. "I'm stuffed, I mean, I've had enough to eat but what would you recommend, Gran? No calories at Christmas!"

"We could split a piece of apple with cinnamon ice cream." I turn to Betty. "One serving, two forks, and two coffees." After Betty clears away our bowls and plates, I look at Phoebe. "Okay, you were worried about me, and I thank you, but I've been worried about you, especially after last night. Do you want to talk about what Mr. Sean had to say? You were on the line for a long, long time. I heard you come upstairs. I couldn't tell if you were just tired or really down."

She rolls her eyes. "If I remember correctly, a little of both."

"He's not the only bacterium in the toilet tank, Phoebe."

She looks startled, then laughs. "Nice talk, Gran."

"You called him a 'turd,' if I recall."

She raises her shoulders in an eloquent shrug. "Don't you believe in second chances?"

"That depends on who is trifling with my granddaughter's heart. In this case, 'no' comes to mind."

She doesn't say anything, but the corners of her mouth quirk in a half smile. I hope she is thinking "Brad."

110

Dessert and coffee arrive. We pick up our forks. As usual, Betty's pie is just this side of ambrosial.

Phoebe makes appreciative noises, sips the coffee. "He wants to fly out for New Year's."

Dammit. I was afraid it was something like that. "Does he have his ticket yet?" I cross my fingers in plain sight.

"I told him I'd ask you first."

"When your mother was in high school, and somebody called her to ask her to do something she didn't want to do, and she didn't have the gumption to say no herself, she'd whisper to me to tell her she couldn't go. So I had to be the bad guy."

Phoebe pulls a face. "Mom's better at saying no these days."

"Having children changes your perspective. The Mama Bear thing."

"I'm not complaining, just making an observation."

"So, what do you *want* me to say?"

"I don't know. How about a nice, definite 'maybe?'" She scoops up the last bite of pie. "Does that work for you?"

"Maybe."

She laughs again and finishes her coffee. I'm so glad she's at least conflicted and not begging me to invite him.

We settle the bill and head for home, with a quick stop at the grocery store. Maybe Brad of the gorgeous blue eyes would enjoy some mulled cider and gingerbread cookies after wrestling the tree into the house.

Phoebe helps me carry in groceries and then tells me she's taking off. "Shopping to do. You're not invited."

She is no sooner out of the house when the phone rings. I check the Caller I.D. Him again. I unplug the answering machine before it can kick in. The phone rings about a dozen times before he gives up.

Smiling to myself, I head back to the kitchen. I soften some butter in the microwave and start the cookie dough. The smell of ginger and cinnamon stirs up so many memories. I am remembering the Christmas of 1944 and how grateful I was for a pound of lard.

Chapter
17

Phoebe and I check the map once more before starting out. She's just come home from an all-nighter history project and can barely keep her eyes open.

"You're the designated driver, Grandmother dear." She yawns mightily. "In the interest of public safety."

"No problem," I tell her. "I love to drive." I especially love driving the wonderful red Jeep I bought, only slightly pre-owned, on a whim a month ago.

We've each packed small bags as we'll probably spend the night somewhere in Vermont. We also brought a cooler of food and water for us and Ringo, who is sitting happily in the back seat, smiling his goofy dog smile. He loves car trips.

The sun shines high overhead in a flag blue sky. The trees are tinged with green. Tulips, blooming in glorious colors, nod in the spring breeze. All in all it's a grand day for a getaway, although I am not at all sure what I have planned is wise. They say you can't go back. Maybe what they should say is, "You're an idiot for trying." Still, I am irresistibly pulled to revisit Camp Chaffee as strongly or perhaps even more so than I am drawn to check out Atlantic Lane.

There's something about a spring day that rekindles the hope and joy of youth. All that newness! Possibilities! Perhaps that's why I am taking this sentimental pilgrimage, thinking to recapture, if but for a moment, the essence of my seventeen year old self.

I'm not even sure I can find Camp Chaffee. Phoebe and I both searched the Internet and found nothing listed. The lake has to be there. Maybe the buildings still remain, although after fifty-odd years, who knows? Winters are harsh in New England.

Springs however are quite splendid. I instruct my distractible self to live in the moment and drink in this beauty as we travel the back roads toward Vermont.

We arrive in the town where Link and I first attended services together and ate pancakes. The fellowship has grown to a full-fledged church, housed in a beautiful stone building. The hotel is still there, but the restaurant where they served those scrumptious pancakes has obviously been razed and replaced with a large sporting goods store. Looking back, I remember the pancakes less and Link's animated face more. True to his word, he didn't propose that day, but by the time we headed back to camp I would have said yes if he had. We didn't marry until just before my junior year. After two lonely years at Gettysburg, I finished my degree at Penn where Link had his first teaching job and completed his Ph.D.

Phoebe is still sleeping, a little scrunched in the passenger seat. Since pancakes aren't an option, we'll eat the sandwiches I packed, once we find the camp, or what remains of it.

I drive well below the speed limit, much to the annoyance of the young man in a blue pickup behind me who is trying to pass, but I can't remember exactly where the camp entrance is and everything is so overgrown. I pull over to let him go by. He honks and gives me the finger. My dear friend, Lois, would probably murmur, "Blessings upon you," and let it go. I however mutter, "Blessings and I hope there's a cop out there to save you from yourself, you dolt." I extend my pinky in his direction in a meaningless gesture that, nonetheless, dissipates my pique and actually makes me smile.

Phoebe wakes up and turns toward me. "Are we there yet?" she jokes.

"We have to be close." I drive another mile and then turn around when I come to the bridge spanning the river that feeds Lake Chaffee. We have gone too far. Now that Phoebe is awake, she can scan the area while I poke along, hugging the shoulder.

113

On the third pass, she says, "Stop. There's a break in the trees. I think."

I pull over. Something feels right. Ringo is eager to get out. I attach his leash, just in case he gets a notion to run out on the highway. He thinks cars are his friends who only want to race, though at ten he's not likely to be much competition.

There's a trace of wheel tracks leading into dense woods. We walk in about fifteen feet and encounter a chain across the overgrown dirt road. Just beyond is a sagging, weather-bleached signboard with the words, barely legible, "Camp Chaffee."

A wave of pain drives tears to my eyes. I hand Phoebe the car keys. Luckily she intuits what I want because I cannot speak. Moments later she returns with her backpack in which she has stowed lunch.

"I locked it," she says, handing me the keys. We step over the chain and start down the trail. "You okay?"

I shrug and try to smile. The pang of loss staggers me, but I soldier on. Deep inside I know I am here to do something. The sunlight filters down through the tree canopy. Birds twitter, squirrels fuss and hurl pinecones and twigs in our wake. Squirrel bombs. Ringo shoots me a woeful look. I bend down and unhook his leash. He wants to run, but he won't go far. These days I am his moorings.

I remind myself once again to live in the moment and soon Phoebe and I are striding along, arms swinging, keeping pace with one another. My spirits lift. I know I will encounter more hard moments today, but for now I will enjoy a hike in company with this beautiful soul, my granddaughter. Our time together is drawing to a close. In another month she will return to Colorado and I have to decide what to do next. I have no idea what that will be, beyond moving closer to Mother.

After maybe half an hour we come to a clearing. I hold out my hand and we stop walking. Through the trees I see the lake gleaming like a mirror on which floats the reflection of a few puffy white clouds. The cabins, now ramshackle, some with caved-in roofs, stand crookedly off to the right. The dining hall is gone, evidently destroyed by fire. Nothing remains but a few charred uprights, a bit of porch railing, and the crumbling stone foundation. Gone. All those people...gone. Many, like Link, dead. But Ringo has seen the water and heads toward it, drawing my attention away from the ruins.

"Well, there's the famous dock," Phoebe says. "Might not be the same one."

"Looks the same. Kind of rickety."

Gingerly we make our way to the end and sit down while Ringo paddles out to be near us. It's too early in the season for me to dangle my feet in the water, but Ringo's a water boy no matter what the temperature. I reach over to touch the post Link leaned against that long ago night. Maybe not the same post, but close enough. Phoebe isn't going to let me get weepy. She opens the backpack and hands me a sandwich. Meat loaf. Part of me wishes it was that nasty mystery camp meatloaf. Given the chance, I would do it all over again, every minute of it.

Smelling food, Ringo seems to be trying to figure out how to climb up beside us. Finally he swims to shore, shakes vigorously, and comes running toward us. Phoebe gives him a dog biscuit. As we sit there a pair of ducks swims by. Perhaps they are the great great great grandchildren of those ducks Link and I watched in the summer of 1950. It goes on, doesn't it? Life, I mean. Without Link, maybe soon without me. Not too soon, I hope. I want to know Phoebe's children.

From the woods behind us comes the sound of an engine ripping through the stillness. We both turn. What appears to be a State Trooper on a motorcycle is heading our way.

"Busted," Phoebe whispers, mischief in her eyes.

"I didn't see any No Trespassing signs, did you?"

"The chain was kind of a clue, Grandmother." She grins at me. "I'll go see what he wants." She jumps up and hurries to meet him.

I get to my feet and follow her.

The trooper is a tall young man, in his mid-twenties. He has a

115

weak chin and skimpy soul patch. Mirrored sunglasses hide his eyes. "Excuse me, ladies, but you're trespassing on private land."

Phoebe smiles up at him. "We didn't mean any harm, officer. My grandmother came here for camp a long time ago and she just wanted to see it one more time."

"Camp's been closed since I was ten years old," the trooper says, but he has obviously noticed how pretty Phoebe is because his grim expression segues into a half smile.

"We came on a sentimental journey. I met my husband here," I put in. "He proposed to me at the end of that dock. He's gone now, almost two years. It probably sounds strange to someone as young as you, but this place has been calling to me and, well, here we are. Even if you throw us in jail, it will have been worth it."

Ringo plants himself between the young man and me and growls a warning.

"Hey, buddy." The trooper looks at me, looks at Ringo, and takes a step back. "He bite?"

"He never has." Phoebe smothers a laugh. I place a hand on Ringo's head. "It's okay, Ringo. Good boy."

"Some kids came in here a couple years ago and set fire to the main building. Could've burned the woods, too, if some guy in a boat hadn't come along and called it in."

"I understand. We'll leave right now. I've accomplished what I came for." Or have I? Something still feels unfinished.

"You aren't going to give us a ticket, are you?" Phoebe asks.

"Probably should," he mumbles, his cheeks turning red. "But seeing that you just came to remember stuff, I'm gonna let it go."

"We promise not to make a habit of it," Phoebe says. "We both live far from here. We won't do it again."

He shakes his head and gestures toward the end of the dock. "You ladies might as well finish your lunch." He climbs back on his motorcycle and leaves in a cloud of dust.

We return to the end of the dock to eat.

Phoebe sticks some potato chips in her sandwich and takes a bite. She smiles. "Did your life turn out at all the way you thought it would when you were young?"

"I never thought I'd be married to a college professor."

"But that's who you were married to, not what you wanted to be. Not what you were. What you are."

Copying my granddaughter I dig into the potato chip bag and stick a few chips in my sandwich. "Girlish dreams back then were tied up in some nebulous person who would be the ideal husband. So I imagined someone handsome, rich, and accomplished. Your grandfather wasn't rich, but he was accomplished in so many ways, and I loved his face. I don't know if he was handsome, but he was beautiful." I take a bite of my potato chip enhanced sandwich. "This is actually quite good."

"Would I lead you astray in matters comestible, Grandmother?"

"You're the only one I know who would use 'matters comestible' in conversation," I tease.

"Takes one to know one," she says, "but let's not get sidetracked." The ducks paddle by and Phoebe tosses them a bread crust, torn in two. They lunge for the treat. "Go on with your story."

"After raising your great uncle, I knew I wanted children, but from the time I was a little girl I dreamed of designing houses. I drew pictures of houses on my homework papers, on the backs of envelopes, in my drawing book. I so wanted to be an architect. Society thought girls couldn't do that kind of work, but it was women, at least in that era, who spent the most time in houses. Who better to know what features a house should have? I would swear the person who designed the kitchen in our first house had never cooked anything. Everything was in the wrong place. I applied to a number of schools. All but one turned me down."

"But you didn't go. Why not?"

"I was married and we lived a thousand miles from the one school that had accepted me." I shrug.

"Life really interferes with your plans, doesn't it?"

I pat her knee. "I'm satisfied with the life I've had. Really."

"Have you thought about what kind of house you're going to

look for in New Jersey?"

"I guess I'll just see what's available. Probably something small, all on one floor. I can still get up and down stairs, but down the road, who knows?" I picture some kind of dreary tract house and roll my eyes skyward.

"Grandpa wouldn't want you to be so sad, Gran. " Phoebe slings an arm across my shoulders. "He wouldn't."

"I'm not sad, sweetie." I hug her back. "That's a lie. I am a bit lost without him, but the main thing now is that I have no idea where to go from here with my life. It all seems kind of pointless."

Phoebe's eyes widen. "I'm having a lightbulb moment as we sit here. You should buy property, preferably near water, and design your own house. After all these years, and all those house books you have in your library, you must know what you want and it would be so much fun."

"Oh, I don't think so. I wouldn't know where to start."

"Start by thinking about the houses you admire. Maybe something spare and Japanese-y. And you shouldn't limit yourself to one floor if you get view property."

"I am not riding up and down the stairs on one of those sidecar geezer thingamabobs."

"I can just see you waving like Queen Elizabeth as you ascend to the observatory wearing a hat of Ascot proportions." She mimics the turning white glove and the chilly smile.

We both laugh. "Maybe I could put in a small elevator. But I don't know much of anything about water and heating. Electricity and windows."

"You could get one of those computer programs that help you with plumbing stuff, but you could design the rooms and the exterior. Don't forget a room for me when I visit."

I have never thought about actually designing my own house, but now that Phoebe has presented the idea, I feel a thrill charge through me. The thought is so right I am almost breathless.

"Phoebe, we have to go to New Jersey before you go back home. There's a house...I hope it's still there...owned by the fruit and

vegetable man, Mr. Nishida. I'd like something like his house."
Suddenly I am remembering the blue tiled roofs Link and I had
seen in Japan. "Plain. Very plain, with lots of wall storage. An
engawa on three sides. A garden. New Jersey's the Garden State,
after all. I'm going to have to sell more furniture. Oh, Phoebe,
you blessed genius." I take her face in my hands and kiss her
cheek. "That is the most wonderful idea in the world. I don't have
to have designed hundreds of houses. Just one small perfect house
will be enough."

She holds up her free hand for a high five.

We gather the remains of the lunch and stuff it in the backpack.
On impulse I make a detour by the ruined dining hall. Part of the
very railing where Link and I first talked hangs down from one of
the uprights, charred at one end. I worry the stick until it comes
loose. This will go somewhere in my new home.

"Trespassing *and* theft, Grandmother. Tsk. Tsk. What's next?"

"Embarking on a life of crime in my old age. Who'd a thunk it?"

We head back toward the road. Ringo prances ahead like a
young dog, his tail a graceful black banner. Phoebe and I swing
along side by side, singing camp songs at the top of our voices.
Life is so full of promise I feel I will burst with it.

We spend the night in a bed and breakfast and early in the morning head for home. I have plans to make.

Chapter
18

I push the wheelchair into the solarium. The rubber tires make an unpleasant sticky sound on the linoleum tiles. Someone must have spilled something, not unusual in this assisted living place where Mother has lived for sixteen years. Through the bank of windows at the far end of the room I can see the garden where a weeping cherry tree blooms in glorious pinks in the morning sunshine.

"Isn't that tree something?"

"Why did you come today?" Mother asks for the third time, paying no attention to the tree.

"I'm selling my house in New Hampshire and moving back to New Jersey to be near you and Dick," I tell her, for the third time, trying to suppress my impatience.

"But what happened to that boy?"

"What boy?"

She sighs and glares at me. "Can't you remember anything, Claire? You know, the skinny one with the beard and all the hats. I thought he was sweet on you."

She means Link. A rush of loss stuns me. "He was my husband, Mother," I manage.

"Was? What happened to him? Did he divorce you?"

"No, Mother. He died, two years ago."

"But he was just a boy," she mutters.

"He was eighty." She's almost right. He's still a boy in my heart.

"I'm cold, Claire," Mother grumbles. I bend down to pull the red plaid lap robe up to her chest. These days Mother is chilled almost constantly. I take her icy hands in mine to warm them. She smells like violets--violet cologne and musty hair.

"Soon I'll be cold all the time," she comments with a touch of rue. "Mamma's in the cold cold ground."

"Oh, Mother, it's too beautiful a day for such sad thoughts."

"I'm almost ready to go," she says as if it were a mere trip to the grocery store. "Almost."

I'm the one who isn't ready. I'm not sure why. Our relationship has always been prickly...but she *is* my mother.

"My blood's gone thin. I'm ninety-five years old. Can you believe it? I can't. I feel more like fifty, as long as I don't look at my hands." Mom picks at the blanket with gnarled, age spotted fingers. She used to be so proud of her beautiful hands. She still has her nails done, polished in a ladylike old rose. "Why is the flag flying? It's not the Fourth of July, is it?"

One of the residents, a veteran of World War II, has insisted on having the flag hung from the deck railing even though no one else remembered what May 8th commemorates. "It's the anniversary of VE Day, Mom."

Mother cocks an eye in my direction. "I'll never forget that day. It was the end of an endless nightmare, as if someone had opened a window that had been shut all those years and let in the sunlight and fresh, clean air. All the struggling, making do, scrimping, patching, doing without...." She shakes her head. "Of course you wouldn't remember. You were only a child."

I am annoyed, but not surprised, that Mother still remembers that time differently than I do. She lived in a world of pain for the duration and in her mind I must have stayed eight years old. After all these years I am still waiting for her to thank me for turning over my childhood to take her place, at a time when Carl's disappearance was as disturbing to me as Dick's worry about Dad and Mother being spies was to him. Of course, it wasn't just her depression. It was collateral damage from war. Still, I long to hear her say something like....

Thank you, Claire. We couldn't have made it without you. What a wonderful manager you were. How proud I was of you.

Get over it, Claire. It ain't gonna happen.

I tell her, "Remember the impromptu parade down Main Street that day? Kids on trikes, bikes, scooters. People carrying flags. Everyone kissing and hugging. School got out early. Mrs. Bell led her fourth grade class out the front of the school and down the street, smiling from ear to ear and cheering."

"Poor woman. Her boy got killed at Pearl Harbor, didn't he?"

"Don't you remember? She didn't hear for a few days. She stayed home from school, afraid he'd been killed, but it turned out he was wounded, too badly hurt to remain on active duty. He came home and helped with the war effort by working for the Monmouth County Red Cross."

"I'd forgotten that," Mother said. "I do remember Mae Bienenmald came to watch the parade...after she got all gussied up in that ridiculous red hat."

I don't recall the hat, but I do remember that she spoiled the day for me by telling someone nearby that she had been right about those Nazis across the street. Good thing they were long gone. How I wanted to smack her in the face. "I despised that woman."

"She was a Tartar, wasn't she?" Mother chuckles. "She tried to tell me your father was carrying on with some woman at work. A lady engineer of all things. Who ever heard of a lady engineer? Well, you didn't, in those days."

"If anyone was carrying on with anyone, it was her husband. Who would blame him?" I want to say that I hope he had found solace in kindlier arms, but stifle the urge. "Dad was working seven days a week. He was too busy and too tired to carry on with anyone...and he loved you." He must have! But of course I don't say that.

Mother tilts her head to one side. "Where has the time gone, Claire?"

"I don't know where time goes, Mother." I wish I did. Maybe I could discover a way to get it back.

"Oh, Claire, you always have some weird answer for everything," Mother snaps. She falls silent, gazing through smeary glasses in the direction of the cherry tree. After a while she looks up at me. "Now tell me why you've come to visit. Is it a special occasion?"

Getting old is pigeon poop some pundit once said. I give Mother a hug. "So I can go look for a new place to live."

"You could live here," she suggests, with a sly look.

"That's a thought." Not a very good one.

I wheel Mother to her room and promise to be back with Phoebe in time for dinner.

* * *

Phoebe, who has driven down separately in order to spend a day with Brad and his family in Morristown, is waiting at the motel. She'll spend a couple days with me hunting for land and then go back to Brad's for a brief second visit, before they both return to New Hampshire to prepare for finals. I know in my head that the time for her to move on is coming, but my heart dreads the separation. What a precious gift her presence has been to me this past year. Thank you, Sean. I don't know if Phoebe's relationship with Brad will turn out to be what she wants, but at least she's well over the other one and maybe a little more able to face disappointment.

We take the sentimental journey before looking for property.

It has been sixty years since I was in Marlsburg, but I have no trouble finding Atlantic Lane. The old house looks pretty much the way I remember it, except they've enclosed the screened porch on the front, the mulberry tree is gone, and the original single garage has been replaced with a double.

I feel a tingle of nostalgia as I turn to look at the Goehners' house. It has been painted a rather peculiar shade of blue with mauve trim. What would Liesl Goehner think of those colors? I think she would probably just laugh.

"That's Carl's house," I tell Phoebe.

"Really!" She unfastens her seat belt. 'Interesting color scheme."

"I wonder if the present owners would let me just walk around in the back yard. I wonder if they have a garden."

"Don't wonder. Ask," she says, getting out of the Jeep.

I follow her across the street, hoping whoever owns the house is at home and doesn't take us for a pair of proselytizers. Phoebe hurries up the front steps and pushes the doorbell. Her face is bright with expectancy.

After three minutes or so no one has answered the door.

A girl about seven or eight appears at my elbow. She is a tiny child with a slight Asian cast to her features. Her light brown hair is pulled up on her head and decorated with some kind of glittery pouf that looks as if it belongs on a fairy princess. She is wearing what looks like a cast-off evening gown. "They're on vacation."

Phoebe bounds down the steps, giving the child a big smile. "Do you know when they'll be back?"

The girl shrugs. "I'm not sure."

"Do you think they'd mind if we took a peek in their back yard?" Phoebe asks. "My grandma used to live across the street when she was a little girl. Her best friend lived in this house. We won't touch anything."

The girl eyes me as if she cannot imagine I was ever a little girl. "If I go with you, I guess it's okay," she says. "*My* best friend lives here, but they went to Canada."

"What's your friend's name?" Phoebe starts up the driveway.

The girl scampers after her. "McKenzie Emma Porter. What's yours?"

"Phoebe Rae Maes." She winks at the girl. "And what's yours?"

I hope her name isn't McPherson or McDougal. This craze of using Scottish last names for girls' first names makes me wonder if there will be a whole generation of females known as "Mac."

"Madison," she says. "Madison Lily Nishida. Isn't that a pretty name?"

Nishida? I hurry to catch up. "I used to know some people by that name. In fact, I was going to look for their house. It's down that way, a few blocks past the school. A Japanese style house. Their names were Paul and Rose. Mr. Nishida used to sell fruit

124

and vegetables from a horse-drawn cart in the summertime. He wasn't married when I knew him. I thought he was pretty old, but maybe he wasn't. If you're related, he could be your grandfather. Well, probably your great grandfather."

Madison spreads her arms wide and shrugs again. "My Aunt Claire lives down that way in a house like they have in Japan, but I don't know anybody named Paul or Rose."

Phoebe looks at me and mouths, "Claire? Cool. I bet she's named for you."

This time I'm the one who shrugs. Wouldn't that be something?

"I could ask my dad, but he's at work and my mom's asleep right now. She was up all night with my brother." She rolls her eyes. "He's such a baby."

I walk to the end of the driveway and look into the back yard, which is an expanse of smooth green grass, with only a small cluster of zinnias in the far corner. I see that the grape arbor is gone. Grapes probably don't live for seventy years. It's all right; they are still growing in my mind's eye.

I picture Carl's mother in a yellow sundress, kneeling in her garden to pull weeds, a floppy straw hat shielding her face. What anguish she must have felt to have to leave her house and garden. I see her laying Stephen on a blanket in the sun, telling me sunshine was good for rashes. I can almost taste her apple cake and hear her telling me that sunshine might be good for my mother. How different all our lives might have been if we hadn't been so afraid of truth.

I want to sit on the grass and wallow in memories, but the owners aren't here to grant permission and I have to make good use of my time.

"Thank you, Madison," I tell her. "If you think she wouldn't mind, I'll go see your Aunt Claire."

She nods. "She's always there. She has to be in a wheelchair. She likes company. She's really my great aunt." She puts her hands on her tiny hips. "She has a big dog. He barks a lot, but he's really nice. His name is Killer." Her smile is impish.

"Thanks for the warning," Phoebe says. "Maybe we'll stop back another time."

Madison stands on the sidewalk, shifting from one foot to the other, watching us drive away. I sense that my eight-year-old self is sitting on the front steps of my old house, reading "Cinderella" and waiting for Carl to come over. I can't quite see her, but I know she is watching us.

* * *

The bushes that used to shield the front of Mr. Nishida's house are gone, as is the barn. Only a few fruit trees remain, but there is a garden, mostly sprouts in early May. A woman seated in an electric wheelchair directs the efforts of a young boy who is gently hoeing around tiny plants.

We walk slowly across the yard. The woman turns her wheelchair and smiles. "You must be the people Madison called about. I sent my dog inside."

We introduce ourselves. Her name is indeed Claire, Claire Nishida. She looks to be in her late fifties. When she hears my name, Claire Walters Hanneman, she claps her hands and smiles. Her eyes glitter with tears.

"I knew it. I knew someday you'd come and I'd get to meet my namesake. My dad thought the world of you. Obviously. He named his only daughter in your honor. Come inside and we'll have tea and you can tell me what brings you here after so many years."

126

Chapter
19

Ringo is waiting for us on the front porch when Phoebe and I arrive home. He is wagging his tail so hard he almost falls over. Evidently he has forgiven me for going off and leaving him with a sitter for a week.

I kneel on the floor and give him a hug. "I've found a wonderful place to build our new house. You and I will have a view of the bay and we'll drive to the beach and take long walks on the sand." Of course he doesn't understand what I'm saying, but he looks at me with such trust I almost weep from gratitude. Instead, I push myself to my feet and haul my suitcase up the stairs, Ringo on my heels.

Today I'll print out the pictures I took during our trip, including the ones of Claire Nishida. What a lovely visit we had. What fun it was to see her pictures of her father and his wife, Josie. Josie was a Caucasian woman, the child of Universalist missionaries to Japan. She attended school in Tokyo until the political situation drove the family back to the States. Funny how life turns out. Mr. Nishida had been of Japanese extraction, but except for a few words of his parents' native tongue, his only language was English. Josie, according to Claire, often struggled to find the correct English word and when she was upset spoke only rapid fire Japanese. Evidently it took the edges off any conflict, because the two of them usually ended up laughing. Claire's brother, William, named after Josie's father, is Madison's grandfather. She will arrange a meeting with him once I am back in New Jersey. It is a connection I am eager to make.

My new house will be about ten miles from Marlsburg. Claire

and I have promised to keep in close touch. She even offered to let me stay in her spare room while my house is being built. I may take her up on it.

How I wish I could see Mr. Nishida once more and thank him for naming his daughter after me. How I wish I could see all of those neighbors who peopled my childhood, to thank them for their many kindnesses during my mother's long illness--with the exception, of course, of Mrs. Bienenmald. Maybe I could thank her for teaching me how not to be. I suppose she was scared and not very bright, but there was no call for her to treat Carl and his parents so cruelly.

I set the suitcase in the corner of my room, wondering what I should do first. Unpack, I guess.

Phoebe appears at my doorway. "Okay if borrow the cordless? My cell's dead." Not waiting for an answer she snatches it up. No doubt she can't wait to talk to Brad which I suppose is as it should be. "I'll go pick up some milk and stuff at the store," she calls over her shoulder as she heads down the stairs.

"Thanks. Don't forget eggs." My bed looks so inviting. I'll unpack later. I kick off my shoes and flop down, feeling rich with memories, even the sad ones, happy with plans, sorry that in a few weeks Phoebe will head back to Colorado.

Ringo settles down on the hooked rug next to my side of the bed. I hear Phoebe's bug start up. In seconds Ringo is snoring and I am drowsily walking through the house I will build. I hear the phone ringing. I am far too comfortable and too indolent to run downstairs to retrieve the cordless. Whoever it is will leave a message and I can call back later.

I snuggle into the lovely Pashmina throw Phoebe gave me for Christmas. Mentally I step through my Japanese style French doors out onto the engawa to look toward the bay. Since it is my fantasy, I paint a lovely gray summer day, misty and too cool for boating. I erase any tugboats or barges so that the silvery expanse of water looks as it would have centuries ago before Europeans invaded this land. My yard is lush with flowers - yellow wild roses, fat white hydrangeas, a swath of pinks, and dozens of true blue bachelor's buttons.

I smile and close my eyes. The kitchen, I decide, will overlook the bay....

Carl

Chapter
20

It is late afternoon. Shadows reach across the yard to where
I've been plucking hornworms off the tomatoes with needle-
nose pliers and placing them in a jar of soapy water. My wife,
Deda, walks toward me carrying a tray with iced tea in tall glasses,
each topped with a round of lemon. At age seventy, she is still
slender and limber, except for a touch of arthritis in her hands.
She is wearing a red sundress and sandals that are almost the same
color.

"All right, Mr. Grumpy," she says. "It's that anniversary, isn't it?
You're thinking about that time again, aren't you?"

She's right. I've been out of sorts all day and didn't make the
connection. You'd think I'd remember what the hell was wrong
after all these years, wouldn't you? I push up from the kneeling stool...my knees "ain't what they used to be"...and grumble a
terse "Sorry" that earns me a raised eyebrow. I don't know why I
always forget and then it sneaks up on me and I hurt her feelings.

Ashamed, I turn away and look around the yard, at the rich green
of the maple leaves, the lush flowers, the ruddy tomatoes. Mama
would have loved this place.

*My God, she cried that night. How can I leave my beans? My
tomatoes? My beautiful carrots? I still hear her dear voice in my
memory. Just before we left, she put her cool hands on my face
and kissed my forehead. "It is all right. Still I have my beautiful boy." She smiled at Papa, tears streaming down her face, and
added, "And my dear husband."*

Rage shoots through me. Those bastards killed her as surely as if
they'd put a gun to her head!

Deda sets the tray on my kneeling stool and puts her arms around me. Her body is warm and slightly damp from the heat and the humid air. I smell her sweet scent—-freesia, I think it is--and lemon, from cutting slices for the iced tea. I have this ridiculous urge to curl up in her lap and cry. But as I am eight inches taller than she and outweigh her by seventy pounds, I pull back, pick up the tray, and head for the picnic table set in the shade of the weeping cherry tree the kids gave Deda for Mother's Day so many years ago.

I place one glass in front of her and sit down. "Thank you, Deeds. This will hit the spot." She reaches for my hand and, once again, I want to cry. Maybe what I really want to do is roar.

"There's only one way to get rid of this pain, Carl, and you know it," she says quietly. "It's been a barrier between you and the children for too long." She looks at me with tenderness and I wonder how it came to be that someone like me receives such grace.

"I can't do that, Deda." My voice betrays me with a thickness that tells of too much feeling. I pull my hand away, take the lemon round off the edge of the glass, and twist it hard before dropping it into the tea, stirring with my finger instead of the long spoon Deda has put on the tray.

"You don't have to tell them out loud, face to face, if that's too painful. Write your story. For heaven's sake, you produced eight textbooks. I remember the praise. 'Professor Goehner writes with authority, deep and broad knowledge of the material, and the occasional touch of poetry.'"

"Deda, look at me. Do you see one of those touchy-feely gut-spilling sensitives? That time, that horror, is best forgotten. Anyway I'm too old to change my ways, even if they aren't considered healthy these days."

"The shame is theirs," she says softly, as she does every August.

From the vantage point of this new century when such things are not judged so harshly, I can agree, intellectually, but my heart seizes up when I remember my parents' humiliation. "When Papa was still alive, a man didn't shed tears and go on and on about how tough things were and how he suffered and could you please give me a hug? He just squared his shoulders and soldiered on."

"Soldiered his way to high blood pressure, ulcers, and early death," Deda says a bit tartly, even for her.

Her frank way of expressing herself is what attracted me from the first time I heard her speak. She's says exactly what she thinks, and trust me, it's rarely what most people expect.

A tightness in my chest stops me from responding. I've been having these little episodes lately. It's probably the anniversary stuff, tension and, dammit, the fear that never quite leaves me.

But I sip the delicious iced tea, smile at Deda, and for a little while the tightness goes away.

Chapter 21

I woke up this morning in a hospital bed with all manner of tubes and gadgets attached to me--let's not even mention the catheter--and could scarcely remember how I got here.

"He was lucky," someone says.

Lucky? I have a fuzzy recollection of lying face down on carpet, bristly, smelling of rug shampoo. People, bustling and hustling, lifting me onto a rolling cart. Lights and sirens. Deda weeping.

White-faced people - my children and wife - stand in a semi-circle at the foot of the bed. Chris and Mike live within driving distance, but Melissa's been in the Chicago area for ten years, Mark in Denver. They must have flown here to say goodbye. I try to call my wife's name. "Edith." It sounds like gibberish. Melissa bursts into tears. What the hell is wrong with me?

Deda understands and comes to the bed to take my hand. "Don't let them scare you, Carl. Dr. Kisling says you're going to be okay."

I nod, but I wonder how true that could be. Why are all four kids here staring at me like I'm already dead? My eyelids droop. I am so tired. From what? Lying in a bed? I want to get up and feel strong, but my eyes close.

When I open them again, it is dark, and the room is empty of people except for Deda sleeping on a cot nearby. I don't want to disturb her slumber, but I am scared. I try to say her name, but all I can produce is a muffled grunt, like you make when your night-mares elicit a scream. She doesn't hear me. I soldier on.

* * *

It has been six weeks since my heart attack. I have lost fifteen pounds, having given up most of my favorite foods. I am allowed a beer a day which I have with dinner.

This morning Deda brought home a dog from the animal shelter. He's a black and white medium sized collie sort of critter with perky ears. Muttley was the name the shelter workers gave this poor guy. They estimate his age at about five. He's supposed to take me for walks twice a day. For that service he gets his meals, his treats, and a plaid dog bed big enough for a Saint Bernard. I don't really want a dog, but Deda is so pleased with him I stifle the urge to yell, "Take him back."

She evidently has anticipated some resistance. "He needs a home, Carl, his person died, and you need someone to talk to while I'm out."

"You want me to talk to a dog?" I say, speaking more slowly than I used to. I don't know why. I don't think it's part of the pathology. I had a heart attack not a stroke. "Maybe we can teach him to dial the phone if something happens to his new person."

"Oh, hush, you old curmudgeon. I'm not ready to part with you." She smiles. "I'll be at quilting group." She hesitates. "I don't have to go." It's her first time out since I've been home. She needs a break and I find I am eager to be alone for a while.

"Go!" I practically shout, impatient, irritable. "Maybe Muttley would like a quilt. With his name on it." Immediately I am ashamed. It's so hard these days. Hard to see Edith wheel the garbage dumpster out to the road when I should be doing that. Hard to be driven everywhere, even though she is a perfectly adequate driver. It annoys the hell out of me to have to think about every bite of food or sip of drink I put in my mouth. I want some pecan pie. With vanilla ice cream. I want a Warsteiner with my *lunch*. "This takes some getting used to."

"Yes," she says.

She's been doing all the work and I'm the one who fusses. "Sorry." I still sound grumpy, but I smile, fakely. I probably look like an ass.

She sets down her quilter's bag and comes over to me. She plac-

134

es cool fingers on my face and with a pang I think of my mother on that long ago night we left our house forever. My beautiful carrots.

"You have Jan's number?"

"I have her number." And you have mine, I think, happily.

She kisses my forehead. "Your new laptop's just waiting for your nimble fingers."

"And my not so nimble brain," I mutter.

She places her hands on her hips. "If you keep that stuff up, I'm going to have to turn you over my knee and paddle you."

"I can hardly wait." We smile at one another, remembering younger days.

"Start with Claire," she suggests. "You don't have to write anything yet. Just think about her."

I hear the garage door open, the sound of the car starting, the garage door closing. I don't want to write about what happened. I want it to go away. The kids don't need to know about those days of hell and death and shame so sharp it still tears at my soul.

Thinking about Claire is better. I tried to find her once, when I was twenty, but the Walters family had moved away while we were gone and I couldn't find anyone who knew where they'd moved to. I even asked *la Bienenmald*, but that sure didn't turn out the way I'd planned!

Claire. I wonder if her mother ever got better. I wonder if she got to be an architect. I wonder if she's still alive. She'd be... seventy-four?

Does she still have Oma's ring?

I have to smile remembering the suspicious look on Claire's face when I offered the ring to her that day in the grape arbor. Looking back, I'm sure she didn't believe for one minute that I had won it at the Penny Arcade, but like the close friend she was, she probably suspected something was wrong. I recall that at some point she asked me about the men in the black car, but I was too proud and too ashamed to explain.

Most likely she saw the pain on my face and had the tact...at age eight!...to trust my real reason for giving her the ring. Not the

bogus engagement. Hell. We were children
But not for much longer.

* * *

Thanksgiving. Chris and Mike are here with their families. Melissa and Mark are coming for Christmas. Don't want to wear poor
ol' Dad out. The grandchildren are in the family room watching
the Macy's parade. Chris is helping Deda in the kitchen. Of all
our kids he's the one who likes to cook. Good thing since he married a woman who doesn't, but she loves to do yard work and he'd
rather not, so it works for them.

Mike and Elise, his bride of less than a year, who's taken his
motherless children under her wing, are out on a walk.

Marlsburg, the name I finally settled on for Muttley the Shelter
Pup, looks at me out of the corner of his eyes, gauging no doubt if
I am going to rise from my recliner and take him outside. After a
while he gives up and with a grunt closes his eyes.

I've been reading about dogs and communicating with them. It
beats brooding and I can do it in my chair. Marlsburg knows quite
a few words, some of which do not bear repeating, but I am going
to try a visualization thing I read about. I don't know if this is supposed to work on sleeping dogs, but I try anyway.

I visualize myself getting out of the chair, reaching for my old
man's cardigan and golfer's cap, taking the leash from the hook in
the hall closet, and heading to the kitchen where we will beg a low-
fat tidbit or so from the cooks, and then go outside.

I visualize him bounding across the yard after a squirrel. I stare
at him, waiting. He pops up, legs spread, eyes wide open, ears
perky. Hmmm. Coincidence or success? "Good boy," I say, as
I am supposed to do. I get up and grab my old man's cardigan
and cap, proceed to the hall closet for the leash, and head for the
kitchen. Mike and Elise evidently have returned from their walk. I
hear talk and laughter.

"Remember how Dad got so upset when Mark wanted to study
law enforcement?" Mike lets out a hoot.

"Just as long as you don't get involved with the...." Chris's voice.

"Goddam FBI," my sons chorus and burst into prolonged laughter.

Well, of course. I hate those God damned fascists. Marlsburg nudges me, but I motion to him to wait. I want to hear what else my sons have to say.

"What was that all about anyway, Mom?" It's Chris again. "The goddam FBI?"

"And that 'rich phony, Roosevelt,'" Mike added. "Dad's always been the fairest person in the world, so why do those two entities get his dander up? Did something awful happen during the war or something? I know Dad's parents came from Germany, but that was back in the twenties, wasn't it? I never knew them, but they were good people, weren't they?"

"Lovely people," Deda says, though she only knew them for a short time before their deaths.

"How come Dad won't ever talk about his childhood? Whenever you ask him anything, he just says, 'Oh,that was a long time ago, before dinosaurs. Before cockroaches.'"

Silence. Deda is no doubt trying to figure out how to respond. Am I putting stress on her because of my silence? What if something happens to her because she's been protecting me and my fragile sensibilities all these years? She's not young any more. Maybe she's right. Maybe I need to tell the story, for her sake.

I barge into the kitchen ready to slay dragons for my lady. "Boys," I say, exchanging tense looks with Deda, "let your mother alone. There's a reason for the way I feel, but I would prefer not to let it spoil Thanksgiving. I'm working on a memory piece - my life is too ordinary for a full-blown memoir - but when it gets transferred from my febrile brain into the beautiful laptop you kids gave me, you will know probably a hell of a lot more than you ever wanted to about me."

Deda's eyes fill with tears and she crosses the kitchen to hug me. "Thank you," she whispers.

Marlsburg butts me with his head. "Excuse me, guys, but my

trusty mutt has to earn his treats."

I grab a plastic bag for poop duty and we head out.

November in New Jersey is a lovely time. There is a softness to the air. Colors are muted. The roses are almost gone, but here and there one blooms. A few gold and brown leaves, limp in the dampness, still cling to their trees. Kids play tag, toss a football, or ride bikes through leaf piles, shouting to one another, their faces ruddy with exertion. Smoke rises from chimneys.

When I was young, burning leaves was standard practice. I remember raking them into piles with Papa and then watching as he bent to hold a lighted match to a dry leaf. You never forget that wonderful smell even though now such an action would get you a reprimand from the fire chief and possibly a fine.

Marlsburg follows a scent trail eagerly, tail wagging, nose twitching—like a pup—though at five he's approaching middle age. "Go for it, Marly. Even middle age goes fast. Too fast."

But it's the early years that tug at me, when I was safe and happy in my child's world. Until they took it away. I never really felt young again.

Part of me wants to keep blocking it all out, but my nose breathes in the bittersweet smell of the decomposing leaves underfoot. I picture our old house back on Atlantic Lane and for a moment or two it is the fall of 1940.

Chapter
22

Okay, you guys, I have turned on that fancy laptop you gave me and I'm going to write my story. This is not one of my textbooks, so don't expect much "flow," or even anything to speak of in the way of organization. I will write just as the thoughts travel from my elderly brain to my feeble fingertips. By way of introduction....

I am Carl William Goehner, Doctor Goehner, as you well know, professor emeritus at Rutgers University. They still trot me out at graduations and such. I am seventy-six years old and I have guarded a painful secret that up until now only your mother knew. Your mother, the goddam FBI, and a certain Mr. Ennis, Director of the Alien Control Unit of the F.B.I. - and they're not talking. Even now those fools claim that it is "a matter of national security," more than sixty-five goddam years later.

I was born to Johannes and Liesl Goehner on May 2, 1932, in Long Branch, New Jersey. My parents were naturalized American citizens of German origin, loyal to their adopted country, but that meant nothing to the goddam FBI and that rich phony, Roosevelt. For the first nine years of my life I lived in a small, middle class kind of house on Atlantic Lane in Marlsburg, New Jersey. We had a nice life. My father worked as a chemist for a petroleum company. Mama was a thrifty but inventive cook and the best mother ever created. The house was always clean and neat, but comfortable. You weren't afraid to sit in this chair, or to use that table, leave out a jigsaw puzzle you were working on or a book you were reading. You did make your bed first thing in the morning, if you wanted breakfast. (Nowadays you're supposed to leave the bed unmade for an hour or so. At least that's what your mother tells me. Something to do with killing off microscopic critters that live in the sheets, who feast on flakes of your dead skin and so on.) Anyway.

My parents gave me the English form of the German names of my grandfathers, Karl and Wilhelm. They wanted me to be a real American. I *was* a real American, because I was born in the United States, but that meant nothing to the goddam FBI and that rich phony, Roosevelt.

These days you'd have to look hard to find in me the boy who lived on Atlantic Lane. No snapshots of me at that age have survived. Not much of anything has survived from that time. Back then I had my father's dark hair and my mother's gray eyes. I was sturdy in build, with big hands, like my father's. I liked the way I looked.

When I think back to the days before it happened, I remember Papa would come home from work each weekday night and ask my mother, "What wonderful dinner do we have tonight, my dear wife?" My parents always spoke English when I was around, even though sometimes it came out a bit stilted. I picked up some German, by osmosis, as a kid. I studied German later; never spoke it well.

But I digress.

Papa would change into old clothes — -back then people didn't have leisure outfits and so on--sit in his favorite chair, read the paper, smoke one cigarette, remind me never to take up his bad habits, and, if it was summer, go outside to check on the progress in Mama's garden. There were few flowers in Mama's garden. After surviving the Depression, she felt she should be growing serious plants, food rather than flowers. Personally I think dahlias are pretty serious plants, even if you might not care to eat one.

On Sundays in summer we drove to the shore to walk along the beach or went to a park to throw a ball around or fly a kite. In winter we built things at my father's workbench in the basement, or, if there was snow, went sledding. My parents weren't religious, but we did go to the Lutheran church for Christmas Eve and Easter services, a kind of tip of the hat to my grandparents and their traditions.

Papa helped me build model rockets when I showed interest at age six. God, but he was patient! I'll bet you kids wish I had been more like him. Back then I dreamed of becoming a scientist who designed rockets that would go to the Moon, to Mars, into deep space. Outer space, as we called it then. When the time came, I chose geology instead, and that's another story.

My parents died a long time ago, Mama, I have always believed, of a broken heart. She loved our little house, our simple, good life, being a wife and mother, until we lost everything including all those years. Papa was like a ghost after she was gone and always bearing the shame. I think he just gave up. He was gone within a year and a half after her death.

One of these days I might drive over to Marlsburg to see our old house. If I ever do, I will park on Atlantic Lane and walk the streets...to the school I attended from kindergarten through third grade, around the block we lived on, peek into Claire Walters's back yard. She was my best friend. I'll stand and glare at the Bienenmalds' old house. No one should treat kids, or anybody for that matter, the way that woman did. Sometimes I like to imagine her up to her neck in a slurry of pig manure. It's childish, I know, but it tempers the rage I feel when I think of her. Your mother says that the poor woman was just reflecting the way she was brought up. I say, quoting somebody — -La Rochefoucauld, maybe?--that after fifty every man is responsible for his face. Every woman, too. You can't blame society or your parents forever. You have to think for yourself, not just swallow the guff "society" tells you.

I'm getting off track again.

The bad times started early one morning in June of 1941. I remember it as if it were last week.

Chapter
23

We spent hours, Mama and I, cleaning up. Afterwards, I went to my fort in the grape arbor where I hid Oma's ring under a board, hugged my one remaining rocket to my chest, and cried my eyes out. I was scared to death that my friend Claire from across the street would come over, even though I had invited her and her little brother to come see my latest rocket. I didn't want her to see me crying like some dumb baby. Even more, I didn't want to have to explain all that had happened that morning, especially why I had only one rocket left. How I hoped none of the neighbors had been looking out their windows. Humiliating, Mama called it. A disgrace. Though I tried to blot out those memories, I couldn't stop from going over everything those men had done.

Minutes after pushing their way into our house before we were barely out of bed, the men told my father, "Okay, Fritz. Get dressed and go to work."

To see fear on my father's face frightened me more than having strangers with hard eyes and mean mouths barge into our home.

"My work doesn't start for two hours." Papa stammered a little. "What do you want?"

"We're going to search your house."

"What do you look for?" Papa squared his shoulders. His cheeks turned red. "How can you do this? What have we done? Where is the search paper?"

"Search warrant, Fritz. We don't need one. FBI," the man who was the obvious leader explained. "Not with Heinz planning to attack us and people like you helping them."

My father drew himself up to full height. He looked as strong and proud as anyone could in rumpled, striped pajamas. I was proud of him. "My name is Johannes Karl Goehner. Not Fritz. I have lived in the United States of America for sixteen years and I am a citizen since 1932. I do not help the Nazis." He put his arm around my mother who was shaking with terror. "I will not leave my wife, or go to work, while you are in this house."

"You're not going to have a job to go to anyway, if we find what they say we'll find."

"Who is this 'they'? What do they say you will find?" Papa asked. "Why do you believe them?"

"That's not anything we have to tell you." The man gestured with his head. "Okay. You can wait on the porch."

"The neighbors," Mama whispered, gesturing down at her bathrobe.

"May first we dress?" Papa asked.

"I don't trust you going anywhere near your rooms," the man said. "Outside."

The men spread out over the house. The tall skinny one, who reminded me of a stork, went down into the basement. The bald one began a systematic search of the first floor, starting with the kitchen. The third man, so wide in the beam he looked like a duck from the back, waddled to the stairs and up to the second floor. I couldn't bear the sight of Mama's stricken face, so I followed on tiptoe to watch what the man did.

He began his search in my parents' bedroom, opening dresser drawers and hurling the contents to the floor. A ring that Oma, my maternal grandmother, had given to my mother bounced and rolled across the floor. I picked it up and hid it in my pajama shirt pocket.

He yanked down pictures, ripping nails from the walls. He pulled the pictures from the frames. Then he proceeded to the closet. Shoes were inspected, shaken, and flung to the middle of the room; clothing yanked from hangers, patted down, the pockets searched. Finally the man scooped the contents of the top shelf onto the floor and kicked through them. I watched, horrified and furious, as the man tore the blue flowers off Mother's dress up hat and pulled them apart. Why was he doing this? What did he think he would find in a hat? I was so angry I thought I would explode.

The man dropped to the floor and looked under the bed. I knew he would find nothing there. Not even a dust bunny. Mother kept the house spotlessly clean. Getting back to his feet he hauled the spread and blanket from the bed, tossing them and the pillows aside, then pushing the mattress to the floor. "Nothing!" he muttered. He picked up a book from the bedside table. "German," he snarled. "Who's this Rainer Maria Rilke? One of Hitler's girl-friends?" The man riffled through the pages.

"Rilke was a poet, sir," I told him. "He died many years ago, before I was born."

The man whirled around and glared at me. "A poet, a man named Maria? Christ!" He threw the book on the floor, kicked it, and started toward the door. "What're you looking at, Kraut boy?"

My mouth fell open. "I am American, sir. I was born in this country in 1932, nine years ago. Here in New Jersey."

The man shrugged and rolled his eyes. "Where's your room?"

Fear clutched at my throat. Would this ugly man tear my room apart as he had done to my parents'? Was there some way to stop him? If I was polite, perhaps he would spare my belongings. "In here, sir."

My room was as tidy as my parents' room, although since I had just gotten up, the bed was unmade. There was one single book on my nightstand, "Paddle to the Sea." A bit young for me at that point, but I had loved the story, especially the pictures, for a long time. And it was American. My rockets were lined up, arranged by size, on the table next to the window. I was so damned proud of my work. What a fool I was. When I saw the man's eyes light up, I thought the guy was impressed.

"What're those for?" He walked to the table and picked up my favorite, a shiny blue rocket with the American flag painted on the side. "You do this, kid? Or your dad?"

"My father helps with the painting, but I build them. The flag is a decal. Please be careful. They're delicate."

"Pretty good for a kid your age," the man admitted. He pulled a penknife from his pocket, opened it, and before I could protest the son of a bitch sliced open the rocket. "You got a radio hidden in one of these, don't you, kid?"

I had a lump in my throat the size of New Jersey. "No, sir. They are just models. Someday I want to design rockets that will go into space, maybe to the moon or Mars. Please don't destroy them. I worked on them all winter. Please, there's nothing inside. I do not lie."

Systematically that bastard cut a slit in each rocket and smashed them with his fist when he found nothing inside. Each knife thrust cut out a piece of my gut. I wanted to beat the hell out of the guy, but I was afraid. Remember, I was barely nine.

"Guess you were right, kid. Nothing inside." He didn't look one bit sorry.

At least my newest rocket was in a safe place. I knew the man would go through my dresser and closet, upend my bed, tear down pictures. I couldn't watch any more. I was so enraged I felt dizzy. Clutching Oma's ring, I walked slowly downstairs as in a dream to join Mama and Papa on the porch. Flour, salt, the small hoard of sugar, cereal...everything that came in boxes or bags...had been emptied on the floor and trampled upon. I tiptoed across the mess, but some of it stuck to my bare feet.

On the porch step Mother sat huddled, her face hidden by the hem of her faded blue robe in a vain effort to disguise her tears. Father stood facing the yard, hands clenching and unclenching. I joined him, taking comfort from the warmth of his body and the faint smell of the soap Mother washed our clothes with. Rinso, I think it was called.

I looked toward the garden with its neat rows of baby cabbages, curly carrot tops, onions, and green beans I helped Mother plant early in the spring. "I would like to kill those bad men," I told my father. "The fat one broke all my rockets, except the one that's hidden."

Papa put his hand on my shoulder. "I am sorry, Carl. I don't understand why they do this."

"Hush," Mother said. "They will hear you."

I remember screaming, in a soft voice, of course, "I don't care. I do want to kill them. I will not always be small."

Moments later the three men emerged from the kitchen, trailing flour and cereal flakes on their shoes. "The garage locked?"

"This is a safe neighborhood," Papa said. "We do not lock our doors."

The tall man laughed. "Maybe you'd better start."

The three men swarmed over our garage like ants on a piece of honey cake, checking every tool, every box, every corner, though the garage was almost as neat as the kitchen had been. They looked through the car, pulling up the seats and rummaging underneath. They dug through the glove compartment and rifled the trunk. Finally, disgusted, they stood in the pale sunshine in the open doorway.

The grape arbor was just to the side of the garage. I held my breath. Would they look in there? Would they find my last rocket? If they touched it, I would attack, punching, kicking, biting, not caring what they did to me.

At last two of the men headed down the driveway toward the car, not even looking at us. The man who had broken my rockets walked up on the porch and poked Papa in the chest with his forefinger. "We didn't find where you hid your equipment, Fritz, but we'll be back one of these days. You can count on it."

"We have no equipment," Papa said. "Any time you come, you will find nothing but our simple belongings."

"That's not what your neighbors say." He held up two photographs he'd taken from the bedroom. "Who are these people?"

"My brother, Heinrich, and my cousin, Kurt. And that one, that is my wife's sister, Christa, and her brother-in-law, Hans Kohler."

"Still in Germany?"

"Yes. Still in Germany."

The man nodded as if they had admitted to a great crime. "We'll just keep these. Maybe you're helping Hitler by sending money or information through them."

"We don't help Hitler," I blurted. "We don't. I am American."

"How would you know what your parents do, little Kraut? You're just a kid."

I thought I would blow up with rage, but Papa's hand tightening on my shoulder kept me from saying anything more.

The man walked away, hands in his pocket, whistling. Whistling, while my mother wept with shame!

Later Papa went upstairs to dig through his clothing to find clothes for work. "I will go as long as I still have a job," he said when he left. "I'll help clean up when I get home, Liesl." He kissed Mama and patted my head. "I am sorry."

"You didn't do anything to be sorry about, Papa."

"No, but I am sorry still for what they did to your rockets. They were well done. I am shamed that I could not stop them. A good father takes care of his family, but I did not dare." He went to the garage, put the car seats back in place, and backed out of the driveway, his face somber, full of pain.

After he was gone, I walked into the kitchen and looked at the mess on the kitchen floor.

"We can do this," Mama said so softly I could hardly hear her.

All morning we straightened up, putting things away, sweeping up the broken things. Mama saved as much of the spilled sugar as she could brush into a teacup. "We must not waste food," she said, her voice thick with sadness and anger.

"Will they come back?" I remember running to peer out the front window at the spot where the car that had brought the men had been parked.

Mama followed, placing her cool, soft fingers on my cheeks. "This FBI, they do just like the Nasos in the old country."

"Yes, but will they come back?"

Again she did not answer my question. "At least," she said, sighing, "they did not touch my garden."

Chapter
24

The night after the men came was one of those godawful New Jersey summer nights. You know the kind. It's sweltering and the air's so sticky the sheets cling to you and it's hard to breathe. Nobody had air-conditioning in those days. Mosquitoes buzzed on the other side of the screen, trying to get at me. I remember perching on the side of my bed and pushing the curtain aside to look down into the yard. Fireflies blinked on and off like harbor warning lights. Idyllic, huh?

My parents had tucked me in at least an hour before. Normally, I conked out immediately--I was a good sleeper in those days--but every time I closed my eyes, I saw those bastards swarming over our house, hurling things from the drawers, trampling through Mama's flour and sugar in the kitchen, going through Papa's car.

Destroying my models.

God, how I wanted to beat those men to a bloody pulp.

To this day I can think of nothing worse than the rage I felt coupled with my child's powerlessness. I tried to think of some way to stop those men, if they came back. I had visions of shooting at them before they even got out of their car and making them drive away. What a joke! I didn't even own a water pistol. My father hated guns. Imagine. A "Nazi" who hated guns.

I'm ashamed to say I cried, again, almost swallowing my fist to keep from howling, so my parents wouldn't hear me. How could I add to their misery? What I couldn't figure out was how those men could do what they did to us. We weren't Nazis. We weren't bad people. We were American citizens, just like them...and they broke my rockets and called my poor father "Fritz." Papa could do nothing to stop them. His shame, Mama's shame, was hell for me to witness.

I cried so much my eyes felt like poached eggs. I remember looking out at the night and dreaming of the day when all this would be long behind us. I would design and build rockets that would head out for one of the planets, Mars, maybe, or one of Jupiter's moons. Maybe I'd be one of the lucky ones who got to go along. I wished I could put those men in a rocket and send them out beyond the farthest planet, where they would freeze solid and never come back. But there were probably many more men just like them.

All I could think of was...what if they came back? What would they do to the rest of the few remaining belongings I cared about?

I can still picture in my mind's eye that last rocket, the silver one I had hidden in the grape arbor, the only one Fat Bottom didn't destroy. Earlier that evening I had set it on my worktable near the front window. The streetlight shone on it and made it seem to glow from inside. If I squinted I could almost believe the rocket was a real one, staffed and ready to head into outer space. I was so proud of the new design. With Papa's help I had painted the fins to resemble grasshopper wings. It was slick!

They will not get this one, I promised myself. Never!

I decided to give the rocket to my friend Claire for her baby brother. All of my rockets would have to live in my head where no one could smash them ever again.

I would give Claire's brother Richard my books, even "Paddle to the Sea." I had no time for baby stories. I had work to do, so those men, if they came back, *when* they came, would find nothing I cared about. Not one damn thing.

* * *

In the next room, my parents were talking softly, in German. I could only catch a few words. I had never wanted to learn German, but now I wished I could understand more of what they were saying. Papa, so quiet and so gentle, spoke in a firm tone. What was he saying?

Mama sounded as if she were gulping tears, talking in spurts, a word or two, then silence. Another word. Papa's name. "Johannes!" What was she saying?

After a long while the talking stopped. The bedsprings squeaked as my parents settled in. "Good night, dear Liesl."

Why had they started speaking English? Did they suspect I was awake and listening? I remember lying down and pulling the sheet to my chin. If they came to check on me, they would find me breathing as if I were asleep, my eyes closed.

As I lay there, fretting and worrying about my parents, I decided that the next day I would ask my mother to start teaching me German. If people were going to call me a Kraut, I had better know how to speak like one. And I had a plan. Two plans. To have plans was the best way to not be afraid.

* * *

In the morning I snuck out of the house after Papa left for work and Mama was in the back yard pinning wash on the line—-she had washed everything those men threw on the floor, including the bedding. With my rocket under one arm and a pile of books under the other I headed for Claire's house. Mr. Walters had left for work, so I knew Claire would be up, taking care of the baby and whatever else needed to be done.

As I crossed the street I heard a door creak in the house next to Claire's. Old lady Bienenmald came out on her porch.

"Hey, you! German boy. Where are you going?"

I kept my head down and pretended not to hear her.

"Don't you ignore me, you rude child."

I stopped then and looked at her with all the scorn I could muster. I wanted to say to her...At least I do not shout at people and call them ugly names, but I would have shamed my parents who had taught me good manners, even if I didn't always use them. I was not going to give her anything to pass on to the neighbors. All she could say was that I had ignored her.

I went around to the back door of the Walters' house and peered through the screen door. Claire's brother, Richard, was sitting at the kitchen table, shoveling Wheaties into his mouth and pretend-reading the cereal box. I knocked. "May I come in?"

"Okay." Richard kept eating. "Claire's feeding Stephen."

I walked into the kitchen and looked around. I remembered from before when Mrs. Walters wasn't sleeping all the time. She would be arranging flowers, or opening a box of bakery crumb cake to share, humming along with the radio and maybe doing a dance step or two. The house was even more quiet than my house had been after those men left.

If she were alive today, she'd be in her mid-nineties. She was a pretty woman until after Stephen was born and she got so thin from not eating.

"Is that rocket for me?" Richard asked.

"I brought you some books. The rocket's for Stephen."

"Stephen?" Richard looked so disappointed I almost changed my mind. "But I like rockets, too."

"I'll make you a new one," I told him, even though I had decided not to make any more rockets until I was sure the men would not return. "A better one. You can decide on the color."

Richard still looked crushed, but he handled it well for a kid of five. "Okay. I'd like a red one. Thanks for the books." He pushed the cereal box away and began paging through "Paddle to the Sea."

I tried not to mind that Richard's fingers were sticky. It was still better than my book being in the hands of those men.

I carried the rocket into the living room where Claire sat holding the baby against her shoulder, patting his back. "I brought this for Stephen." I set the rocket on the coffee table. "I guess it's a dumb present for a baby."

Claire smiled at me as if I were Santa Claus. "It's a lovely present, Carl. Stephen doesn't need any more receiving blankets or stuffed animals." She looked at me with a puzzled expression. "Why are you giving away your rocket?"

I sat on the couch, hands tucked between my knees. I wanted to explain, but I didn't know what to say. For some reason, I was ashamed, afraid I'd cry. I was ashamed of that, too.

Claire continued to pat Stephen's back. "Who were those men who went into your house the other day? The ones in the big black car."

I felt like I'd been punched in the gut. "Nobody," I lied.

"Carl, I saw them. Everybody saw them. They weren't 'nobody.'" Stephen lifted his head and let out a ringing burp. Claire held him away from her shoulder and smiled at him. "Good boy."

I remember thinking that nobody would say that if I made such a noise. Sometimes, in the grape arbor, when Mama couldn't hear, I used to belch and recite as much of the alphabet as I could say while the belch lasted. Once I made it to "n."

"How's your mother?" I asked, to change the subject.

Claire shrugged. "Every day Dad says he thinks she's a little better. He just hopes she's better. She isn't, really." She settled Stephen into the crook of her arm and put the bottle nipple against the baby's mouth just like a real mother. When he sucked it in, she said, again, "Good boy."

I remembered Mrs. Bienenmald yelling at me for no reason. "Why do grownups always say 'good boy' to babies and 'bad boy' when you're not a baby anymore?"

Claire shrugged. "My grandmother says I'm a bad girl every time she calls. I wonder what she would say if I didn't help. She acts like it's my fault Mom won't get out of bed." She sighed. "I hate it when they say I'm bad, especially when I'm doing my best. And then they say, 'Well, you're just a child,' as if being a child was like being the worst criminal in the world. Like being Hitler." She wiped a dribble of milk from Stephen's chin with a wash cloth. "When I have children, I'm going to always tell them they're good."

"Even when they're bad?"

Claire raised her eyebrows and pushed her bangs out of her eyes. "Children are not bad. Just naughty sometimes. I'm not sure what to do about that. Maybe I could just make them stay in their room until they were good."

"That might be a long time. They might starve to death if they're like Petey Merino," I said, trying to make her laugh.

It worked. She laughed. "He's almost asleep. I hope he'll take a long nap today, so I can get something done around here."

It was no fun now that Claire couldn't ever play anymore. I felt like going upstairs and telling her mother to get up, but, of course, I didn't. It wouldn't have helped anyway.

It's funny how I can recall everything that happened that day, as clearly as if it were this morning. Claire got out of the rocking chair and laid Stephen in the carriage which, for some odd reason, was in the living room. She covered him with a knitted blanket, blue and white striped, and tucked it around him. She really did love that baby.

"Come on, Carl. You can talk to me while I do the dishes."

Richard was putting his bowl in the sink when we entered the kitchen. "I'm going outside," he told us. "Joe Clark Bar and I are going to kill some more Germans." He stiffened and looked at me in a funny way. "Not you, Carl. We like you."

"I am not German," I told him.

Richard shrugged. "Mrs. Bienenmald says you are. She says your father's a spy. She told Mrs. Merino the FBI was in your house and they found a picture of Hitler."

"There was no picture of Hitler," I cried. "*She's* the spy. She's always peeking out the window and looking where she has no business looking." Could she have been the person who called the government to tell lies about my parents?

Claire climbed onto the stepstool in front of the sink. "Mrs. Bienenmald is a witch. She's a mean old ugly horrible liar and I hate her." She sprinkled soap flakes into the dishpan and turned on the hot water. "If I had a magic wand, I'd turn her into a toad and run over her with my bicycle." Claire meant to make me feel better, but I knew she would never run over any living thing on purpose, not even an ant. But I loved her for saying what she did.

She stirred the hot water with her hands to dissolve the soap. Her hands turned bright red. I wanted to tell her about the men, about the real reason I had given her Oma's ring, but the words stuck in my throat. To talk about it made the humiliation even more real. If I told about how that man broke my models, for sure I would cry. "You still have the ring, don't you?" I hoped the question would make her forget what Richard had said about the FBI guys being in our house.

"Of course I do. It's in my top dresser drawer, behind my socks, if you don't believe me."

"I didn't mean it that way." At least one of Oma's rings would be safe from those men, even though I hadn't given it to Claire for that reason. Not exactly. I thought it was funny that she was learning to cook from Mama, even though it wasn't because we were engaged, but because someone had to fix food for her family.

I watched Claire rinse a cereal bowl and set it on the drain board. Poor Claire had so much work to do. I grabbed a dishtowel someone had hung on the back of a chair, picked up the bowl, and wiped it carefully. We got into a rhythm of her washing, me drying.

"Carl," Claire said, in a voice that sounded like a grownup, "were those men really from the FBI? I won't tell anybody. Cross my heart and hope to die."

I was about to run out of the house when someone knocked on the back door. "Claire, dear. It's Mrs. Bienenmald. I brought you some homemade peanut butter cookies." Her fake sweet voice made me sick.

Claire turned to me and crossed her eyes. I had to put both hands over my mouth to keep from laughing out loud.

Mrs. Bienenmald opened the door and came inside carrying a plate with an old cloth napkin over it. The glare of disapproval she turned on me faded away when Claire turned around. "These are for after dinner," she said with this phony smile. "For *your* family."

"Thank you, Mrs. Bienenmald." Claire stepped off the stool and took the plate. She set it on the kitchen table. "That was very kind of you to go to all that trouble."

For a witch, I thought.

"No trouble at all." Mrs. Bienenmald kept running her hands over her flowered apron. "I heard your mother calling you, young man," she told me. "I should think you would have something better to do at home than to bother poor Claire when she's so busy."

"He was helping me," Claire said, again in her grownup voice.

Mrs. Bienenmald snorted. Something flew out of her nose and landed on her apron. "He has a mother who needs his help."

I forced myself to have no expression on my face. I folded the dishtowel and hung it back on the chair. "See you, Claire." I left through the kitchen door, taking care not to let the door slam.

There were too many things kids didn't have control over. I promised myself that from then on, no matter what happened or how mean people were, even Bienenmald, I could have control over myself.

No one would ever take that away. Ever!

My mother said she hadn't been calling me.

* * *

Two weeks later the men came back during the day when my father was at work. The bastards. They found nothing of mine—-not one solitary thing--to wreck, but they left the house in shambles again and my poor mother trembling on the back porch, her apron flung over her head.

Chapter
25

“ They came at night, on the twentieth of August, six of them, carrying machine guns.

Machine guns!

Can you imagine such a thing? I thought they were going to kill us then and there.

Thank God, at least they came after dark so the neighbors couldn't see them.

We were given a box each, the size of a suitcase, and one hour to pack. You can't get much in a container that size. We took mostly clothes.

One of the men had been to our house before. Of course it was the fat guy who broke my rockets. He followed me to my room to watch me pack, probably worried I'd get on my short-wave radio and notify Nazis in jack boots to come quick with guns blazing, shouting "Heil, Hitler!"

I, of course, had nothing but clothes to pack.

"No toys, kid?" He actually had the nerve to ask me that!

"Don't you remember?" I said in as snotty a voice as I dared. "You broke them all." All except one, which was safe with Stephen Walters and which I never saw again.

My parents acted like characters out of one of those weird avant-garde movies from the sixties where nobody had shadows, wandering around like automatons, picking things up, putting them down, trying to decide what they couldn't leave behind. Mama took the tablecloth my grandmother had embroidered for their wedding present and some clothes. Papa took his violin and a small clock that had belonged to his father. He forgot his razor. He had quite a beard before he managed to get another one. More about that later, when we get to Texas. Yes, Texas.

Mama, somehow, found the energy to worry about Claire. She had me sneak outside and hide her cookbook and a note for Claire in the grape arbor while the self-important bastards were posturing like a bunch of stuffed oxes in the living room. FBI. Effing Bureau of Imbeciles! I added a quick note to Mama's. "Don't forget me. Your friend, Carl."

I have wondered over these many years if she ever found the cookbook or the note. I hope she did. Even more, I wonder if she saw the men and the guns. She might have since her bedroom looked out onto the street. What must she have thought of us? If she saw anything, she'd remember *me* all right. As a criminal. As the child of Nazi spies. Even though none of that was true.

I didn't know the word at the time, but now I would call that entire experience "surreal." Your whole life is turned upside down and inside out. Everything you have known all your life is taken away, just like that! A snap of the fingers and your childhood is gone and you find yourself being carried away in a convoy of cars to a place where there is no one you know, and your beautiful mother is put somewhere else.

We were in the men's quarters, but they wouldn't even let me stay near Papa. For God's sake, I was nine years old. For a while I was the only kid in the place. They gave me a cot in another of the big sleeping rooms between two cranky old men who called me "little snot nose," and then they'd laugh. I don't blame them for being cranky...in their place I would have been mad as hell...but the nickname enraged me. I always used a handkerchief. Well, it gave them something to laugh about and the offense took my mind off the really bad things that were happening to me.

All this took place months before Pearl Harbor and the massive round up of German Americans after Hitler declared war on the United States on December 11th. A short while later Italian Americans were interned as well. Sal Marinaccio, one of the kids I knew slightly from Cub Scouts, showed up. Well, he was American born, like me, but that carried no weight. They interned Italians, too.

I have never found out why us, why then. The United States wasn't yet at war at the time we were taken! In all these long years no one has ever apologized to us, let alone acknowledged what happened. At least the Japanese Americans got a belated apology, after half of them were dead, and a pittance for all they lost. I don't begrudge those people a thing, but why couldn't the government have admitted what they did to us as well? I don't need their goddam money.

Starting in '42 some of the interned German-Americans were shipped to Germany to be exchanged for Americans trapped there by the war. I was scared to death they'd send us. Some internees remained in captivity until 1948 (they let us out in '47), three years after the war ended! And they had never been convicted of any crime against the U.S. or anybody else. They were forced to sign secrecy oaths and threatened with deportation if they told anyone what had happened to them. Many, including my parents, went to their graves bearing that secret, that shame...and that rage. Okay, kids. That's it for tonight. I can't do this anymore."

I turn off my laptop and look up. Deda, on the twin couch across from me, is smiling warily. "I love you," she says.

I try to tell her I love her, but I am engulfed by a flood of tears. I am sobbing, hiding my face in my hands. In a moment she is up and around the table, kneeling on the couch beside me. She holds me in her arms, rocking me like a baby.

I realize she is crying, too. Her tears fall on my bald spot and run into my hair. She produces a tissue from somewhere...a sleeve or a pocket...and dabs at the wet stuff.

For some reason this strikes us both funny and suddenly we are laughing like a pair of idiots. When things subside a bit, she leaves me, promising to be right back. She returns with two small glasses of brandy. We clink our glasses.

"Thank you," she says.

At last I am able to speak. "I love you."

"I know," she says.

Chapter
26

After Deda leaves for her quilting group in the morning, my head is swimming with memories. Feelings bubble up; images stream across my mind like a movie I saw a long time ago, a black and white film with occasional blips of color. Oddly I am eager to get to work.

I intend to head for the study where my laptop awaits, but Marly, as Marlsburg has become, waits at the kitchen door, practically tap-dancing in his eagerness for the morning walk. I bundle up and off we go.

It's a pleasant day, sunny, cloudless. The January thaw is in full swing. I know we have another month or two of winter, but gardening thoughts temporarily replace my war memories. When we get home, I give Marly his biscuit, fill a mug with hot coffee and a dollop of forbidden cream, and head for the den where my nine-year-old-self waits for me.

* * *

Through the tall windows I watched the gray rain falling almost sideways in the wind. No one would go outside today. The exercise yard was a gloppy mess of mud and brown puddles. I shivered in my thin polo shirt. I had loved that shirt, a blue one with gray and white stripes, when we first bought it. Many washings had turned the colors dingy and, with only short sleeves, it was not warm enough for November. I was growing out of it but I wanted to put off wearing those olive drab shirts they issued the other internees as long as possible. Huddled against the cold, I tried to decide which was worse, never being warm, never being alone, always feeling hungry for home cooking, or every minute missing

Mama so much I wanted to hit somebody.

From my cot I watched the men pace, smoke, stare out the windows, punch a fist into the palm of the other hand, exchange sour glances with each other. A few played checkers or cards. One man carved on a deer horn, whistling softly. Another waited with a rolled-up paper for any cockroaches that showed themselves, pouncing on them and shouting, "Gotcha!" Papa sat alone on the far side of the room, chin in hand. He no longer smoked to save what little money he still had. What was he thinking? Was he dreaming of home, too?

I climbed off the cot and started toward him. If I sat next to Papa I wouldn't feel the cold so much.

"Where you going, little snot nose?" one of the men called after me. The other man cleared his throat and spat phlegm into a napkin.

To get away from you, I thought. I didn't dare say anything but, childishly, I wiggled my bottom at them. They roared with laughter.

Papa looked up when I approached and smiled sadly. It was strange to see him dressed in tan work clothes and the heavy brogans he'd been issued. "Forgive me, Carl," he said.

I snuggled against him. "You didn't do anything."

Papa made a gesture that took in the room, the shabby furnishings, the muddy compound. "You should be in school with your friends, with Claire, learning the things you'll need to know when you are a man." He bowed his head. "Nothing I learned in school could have prepared me for this."

"We'll be home in no time," I said, hoping to comfort him. "Won't we?"

We will be home here before winter, you'll see, Mama had said the night we were taken away, as if she really believed it. Where had they put her? When would I see her again? Mama. I bit my lip to keep from crying.

Papa tugged at my shirtsleeve. "You shiver. I am sorry. We did not know to bring warm clothes. It was summer and so very hot. We did not dream we would be still here in winter and there was not so much room in the small boxes." He rubbed at his beard and put his arm around me, pulling me close to him. The warmth of his body felt wonderful, though his fingertips left icy points on my arms.

My thoughts traveled home again. By that time of year most of the leaves would have fallen. The frost would have killed Mama's garden and birds had probably eaten all the grapes, unless Claire had come to pick them. I hoped she had. Then she would have found Mama's cookbook and my note.

To forget where we were I pictured myself climbing the stairs to my room. In my mind I saw the blue curtains Mama had embroidered with little red and white sailboats. I imagined the photographs of mountains (American mountains!) on the wall. If only I could be in that room right now, warm and happy. I would wave across the street to Claire. She would come over and we would play Parcheesi or rummy and have apple cake with milk.

"Our house will still be there when we go home, won't it?"

"The house will still be there," Papa said in a voice so hard and angry I scarcely recognized it.

The realization of what he was really saying made my head swim. Our house will be there, but it won't be our house any more. I looked up at his tired face. His eyes were rimmed red and bloodshot. My heart broke into a thousand pieces. "How do you know it won't be ours?" I demanded, furious.

"They made me sign a paper, Carl. I had no choice."

"Did they put us here so they could steal everything? Why didn't they take rich people with big houses?"

"They put us here because they do not really believe in what the Constitution of the United States promises all citizens," Papa said. "Only when it is convenient. Taking our house and car, well, that was just extra."

I made fists, ready to fight. "I hate them. I hate them, Papa. I wish I could kill them. Maybe you should not have come to this country. Maybe it is not such a good thing to be American if they treat us like that and steal our house."

Papa patted my arm and pulled me closer. "It is even worse now in the Old Country. Do you forget that there is war there? That crazy Hitler is a dangerous man. He makes life hard for all Germans. People go hungry and now I read in the newspaper that they make the Jews wear yellow stars on their clothing so everyone will know what they are and won't speak to them or patronize their shops."

"But that's mean. Why do they do that, Papa?"

"I am not sure why that evil man wants these things, but I do know that it is not a good time for any Germans, especially the Jews."

"The Nasos are bad people then, aren't they?"

Papa shrugged. "No one is all bad. Surely they love their children."

I thought for a minute. "We're not Jews, are we?"

"No."

"Does that mean we're not anything, then?"

"We are human beings, Carl. We deserve respect and fairness. That is what they pretend not to see. They lock us up like criminals or dogs in a pen."

"But why?"

"Because they are afraid." His breath tickled the top of my head.

"Of *us*?" I slumped, placing my hands between my knees to warm them. "I'm afraid of *them*."

Papa nodded. "I, too. They do what they want and then make up a reason for it."

"Then what can we do?"

"We wait, we keep informed, and, if things go well, when times are good again, we vote." Papa stood up. "You must learn somehow, Carl. Come on." He walked over to the guard who sat smoking and reading the newspaper. I followed. "Excuse me, sir, but my son is the only child here. He is an American, born in this country, but he is not going to school. I have paid taxes to this country for many years. Surely there is a way for Carl to have books and paper."

In later years they held classes for the interned (American!) children, but for me, that time marked the end of formal schooling for several years.

The guard put down the newspaper, exhaled some smoke, and studied me through scratched glasses. "How old are you, kid?"

I squared my shoulders. "Nine. And a half."

"Fourth grade?"

"Yes, sir." I should have been in Mrs. Bell's class with Claire and the other kids. They would be studying about Egypt if they did the same as last year, and learning fractions. Playing dodgeball on the playground. Making dumb turkeys out of pinecones and colored paper for Thanksgiving. Even that would be better than this.

Thanksgiving. What a laugh. Thanks for nothing.

"I have a little money," Papa said. "To pay for pencils and paper."

"Keep your money, Goehner. My wife's sister's a teacher. I'll ask her to get some used books and other supplies for your boy," the guard said, not unkindly. "Kids need something to keep them out of mischief."

What kind of mischief could I have gotten into in that place?

"Men need something, too," Papa said. "Not carving on wood or deer horn, although that is better than just walking around wearing out your shoes."

Books! Paper! I could hardly wait.

Another week passed before the guard came back with a brown paper bag filled with books, lined tablets, a box with gray pencils, a sharpener, and a big pink eraser.

After thanking him over and over, I carried the bag to a table and took out each book, one at a time. It felt like Christmas only much better. There were books for social studies, science, reading. A book for arithmetic. A book about cowboys. Even though the books were used and worn, one without any cover at all, I was thrilled. I pulled out the last one and grinned up at Papa. "I never thought I'd be this happy to have a spelling book."

He laughed, a real laugh, and tousled my hair. "At least you keep a sense of humor. Shall we start then with spelling since you are so happy?"

Horrified, I exclaimed, "Spelling last. Arithmetic first."

"For when you are a famous scientist?" Papa teased.

"Someday I will make you proud of me."

"Already I am proud of you, Carl. Now, let us start with this problem. Two cars are heading east. One car...."

"Oh, that's easy." I grabbed a tablet and pencil and got to work, happier than I'd been since that day last summer when the FBI men came for the first time. I made a promise to myself I would get back at them for what they did to my family. Then I went to work on those word problems. I would not be locked up forever.

Chapter 27

❝ ❝ Kids, this next part of my life is a rough one for me to even
think about, much less share with you. It was a time of rage,
powerlessness, and despair, but I don't want you feeling sorry
for dear ol' Dad. I got through it because of my very wise parents
and the memories of my childhood friend, Claire. During our
sojourn in that godforsaken place my father taught me the meaning
of compassion, even in the face of great evil."

Doesn't that sound melodramatic as hell! Thank the engineers
for the delete button! Poof! Start over.

I reach for my coffee mug and take a sip. The coffee is already
cold, but I am too indolent to take it to the microwave for reheat-
ing. Instead I look out the study window and contemplate my yard
and garden. What a joy to live in a place where the temperatures
are mostly moderate and the rainfall is generous.

Winter is losing its grip. The tips of daffodils and tulips bulge up
from the garden beds. Spring has cast a hint of green, or perhaps it
is only the hope for it. How I dreamed of growing things, of home
and Mama's garden, in that hot, desolate place twenty miles from
the Mexican border. How I missed my best friend.

"July 27, 1942
XXXXXXXX Texas

Dear Claire,

I'm ten now. Where we live used to be a prison for ladies.

At least we are all together again, even if we only have two ugly rooms and no bathroom or kitchen. Papa bought some paint and Mama made curtains and we all cleaned a lot, so it doesn't look or smell as bad as it did the first day. One thing is funny. There are crickets everywhere. Some of us boys chase them around in the showers. It's really hot here, much worse than at home, and no trees anywhere.

I keep thinking about how we used to do jigsaw puzzles and play games on your front porch. I wonder if you found Mama's cookbook. We had to leave so fast and I still don't know why, but I think the witch lady next door to you had something to do with it. Nobody will tell us anything.

I am learning more German. I am scared they will send us to Germany. I have never been there and I don't want to go where the fighting is, but my mother is very sad here.

If you get this letter, please write back and tell me how everybody is. How was fourth grade? Did you have a birthday party for Stephen? With cake? Who is living in our house? Never mind. I don't want to know.

Your friend, Carl"

I remember folding the letter carefully and slipping it into the envelope Mama had left for me before she had to go to her work at the camp kitchen. I wrote Claire's name and address on the front. I didn't know what to put for a return address. Hell, maybe. I had the three penny stamp, but first the letter had to be checked by the people who ran the prison. Only you couldn't call it a prison. You were supposed to call it a camp.

But in my mind it was camp...for prisoners.

Someone knocked at the door. It was my friend Kenny Muraka-mi. He was one of the Japanese Americans in the same camp. I

166

met Kenny almost the first day we got there- — our fathers were on a work crew to build houses for the internees--and we were friends from then on. He was the funniest kid I ever knew. I've always wondered what became of him afterwards. Maybe in this Internet age I could find him.

Kenny poked his head in our door. "Hey, Carl. You want to go watch the basketball game? Come on. It's you Germans against us Japanese."

I remember how angry that made me. Kenny was American born, too, just like me. Nisei was what Japanese Americans called people like him, children of immigrants from Japan. Kenny's parents had wanted to become citizens, but weren't allowed to for some stupid reason. When I asked why, Kenny insisted he didn't know.

"German *Americans*, Kenny," I told him in a not very nice way. "Japanese *Americans*."

Kenny's wheat-colored face flushed. "I know," he said in a sad voice, "but, come on, it's more fun watching a basketball game than peeing on crickets. At least it lasts longer."

I couldn't help laughing. My sour mood vanished like vapor in the Texas sun. "I wish I could pee all day long and drown every cricket in Texas."

"Boy, I'd like to see that," Kenny said with this big grin on his face. "You'd have to drink an awful lot of water first. Maybe we could put a hose in your mouth. In one end, out the other."

We both laughed again.

"Sorry for yelling," I apologized. "I was writing a letter to my best friend from where we used to live. I wish I could be there instead of here."

Kenny made a face. "Yeah. I'd be swimming in our pool right now. I hate this place. It's so hot I feel like a French fry."

Kenny's family had owned three laundry/dry cleaners in California and a large house with a swimming pool. They had even had a live-in maid. All they had left now was their clothes and some kitchen stuff they couldn't even use here.

"It's way too hot." I picked up the letter. "I'll drop this off on the way. No point in wasting a stamp until I know they'll let me mail it."

Kenny reached into his pocket. "I saw your mom in the dining hall. She took me into the kitchen and gave me these." He pulled out two large cookies. "They're oatmeal with raisins." He handed one to me.

I held the cookie to my nose. It didn't smell like the ones Mama made at home with real butter and fresh eggs, but it was better than nothing. I flicked off a bit of pocket lint and bit into the cookie. It wasn't that bad. "Thanks, Kenny."

On the way to the camp office I shuffled along, munching the cookie and stirring up dust with my old shoes, which were too tight for comfort. Pretty soon I'd have to go barefoot. "I wish my mother didn't have to work in the kitchen." The broiling sun made me squint.

I remember feeling very uneasy as I watched the armed guards that patrolled the compound on horseback. They would shoot anyone who went too close to the barbed wire fence. I had this crazy notion to run toward the fence just to taunt them, but then I imagined Mama weeping over my dead body, full of bullet holes and dripping blood all over the place, and decided to ignore them. Someday I'd get back at them. Of course, I never did. It was a child's dream of revenge and those guys are probably long gone from this Earth by now.

"Your mom is a delicious cook," Kenny said, patting his belly and rolling his eyes.

Even after knowing Kenny for months I was fascinated by his eyes, the way the eyelids sort of drooped down, making them look slanted. Epicanthic fold, but I didn't know that expression back then. They weren't really slanted but they were as dark as the coal my family used to have delivered in our old house, when we were still regular people.

Kenny kicked at a stone and sent it flying into a clump of prickly pear. "You know what I wish? I wish my dad didn't have to work in the laundry. He used to be the boss of everybody. He wore a suit and tie to work. Now he wears those dumb brown shirts and pants. It stinks to high heaven."

"Everything stinks here."

"Yeah."

The basketball game ended in a tie, but no one wanted to play overtime in the heat. The Japanese players headed for their part of the compound; the Germans and the few Italians headed back to theirs.

"I hope there's something good for dinner," Kenny said. "I'm starving again."

"Keep hoping," I joked. "It's probably cricket stew. Even my mother couldn't make crickets taste good."

Kenny snorted. "Yummy, yummy, for my tummy. Creamed cricket legs on toast with frog eyes for dessert. See you later, Carl." He took off at a run.

I stopped at the office to pick up my letter to Claire. I didn't even look at it and when I got back to our place, I tossed it on the table Papa had made from a wooden pallet.

Papa looked up at me with a pleased, but solemn expression. In front of him was a bowl of water, a shaving brush, and a safety razor. "At last I can get rid of all this fur." With scissors he cut his beard as close to the skin as he could. "Your mother will be pleased to see my face again, I think, instead of a wild man from the caves."

"I like the beard," I told him. "It makes you look like a man from frontier days."

"It feels like wire and I am tired of the itching," Papa said, making a lather with soap and his shaving brush. He spread it into his beard. "I give it a few minutes to soften the wire."

After Papa started shaving, I got up my nerve to pull the letter out of the envelope. More than half of the words had been cut out, probably with a razor blade. I thought my heart would shatter.

169

"July 27, 1942

████████

Dear Claire,

I'm ten now. Where we live ██████████████████
████████████████████ *we* ████ *have*
two ████ *rooms* ██████████████████ *. Papa*
bought some paint and Mama made curtains and we all
cleaned a lot, ███████████████████████
██████████ *. One thing is funny. There are crick-*
ets everywhere. Some of us boys chase them around in the
showers. ████████████████████████████
████████████ *.*

I keep thinking about how we used to do jigsaw puzzles
and play games on your front porch. I wonder if you found
Mama's cookbook. ██████████████████████
████████████████████████
████████████████████████
█████████████ *t*

████████████████████████
████████████████████████
████████████████████████
█████████████ *.*

If you get this letter, please write back and tell me how every-
body is. How was fourth grade? Did you have a birthday
party for Stephen? With cake? ██████████████
████████████████████ *.*

Your friend, Carl

I crumpled the letter and hurled it at the wastebasket, fighting tears. "Damn them." I knew Papa would be angry at such language, but I couldn't help myself. "They cut out almost everything. I didn't say anything that would help the Nazis. Nothing."

Papa ignored the "damn," but his eyes were sad. He reached down for the letter and smoothed it out. He tried to read it and shook his head. "Tell me the rest, the part they cut out."

I took the letter and read it aloud. When I had finished, I looked up and saw that where Papa's beard had been the skin was fish belly white. The rest of Papa's face, his ears, and his neck was the color of old brown shoes.

"You wrote a good letter, Carl, and you are right. There was nothing in this letter for the Nasos. Even if there are spies in America, and I am sure there are some, I do not think they take the time to look at letters to little girls. But here the people are afraid and maybe they are ashamed about what they do to us. I hope they are at least a little ashamed." He reached for me and gave me a big bear hug. "War makes people stupid."

"Stupid people like war," I muttered. "Stupid old ones who don't have to fight and get killed and lose their legs and arms and get their eyes shot out." Papa's warning pat on my arm shut me up. You had to be careful what you said, even in your own house.

"War is more exciting than the boring day to day life most of us live, but, this time, I am sorry to say I believe it is necessary to fight. I hope and pray that we win, because if Hitler is the victor, the future for Europe and for us is very dark."

In my mind I pictured our old house and yard. How beautiful it had been there. "I don't want exciting. I liked the life we lived. It wasn't boring."

"I, too, Carl. Someday we will have it back."

"It won't be the same, Papa. They took our house, our car, and our furniture." And we lost our friends.

I knew I would never write another letter to Claire.

"Someday we will leave this place and start again with a new house and a new car. You'll see."

"And find Claire?" One thing had been bothering me for a long time. I had never told Mama what I did with Oma's ring. She had not asked, but I doubted she had forgotten about it. She probably thought the FBI guys took it. It was tempting to let her go on thinking so.

"And find Claire," Papa said. "For now, at least, we have each other."

"But we still have to stay here in this ugly place with guards and the school stinks and we're prisoners. Prisoners of war, no matter what they try to call it."

Papa bowed his head over folded hands. "Someday they will realize what they did and apologize. We cannot waste our time staying angry, because then *they* win. We must be strong and we must be kind to everyone, even to those who have put us here because they are afraid. And always we look for something good to hold onto, to be grateful for, even if it's very very small."

"Like what?" I demanded. "What's good about anything here?"

"Like the beautiful morning glories your mother planted to make some shade for us on these hot days." Papa got up and carried the bowl outside where he poured the soapy water on the plants that climbed up strings to the roof. "These flowers did not ask to be planted in this terrible place, so we must care especially for them." He came back inside, wiped the bowl with a rag, and put it away. "Shall we go now for dinner?"

Papa was right. We must be kind. I had an idea. "In a minute, Papa. I need to use the bathroom."

"I wait for you here."

I grabbed the broom and headed out.

"You are flying to the latrine then, Carl? Like a witch?" Papa called after me, laughing, like before, during the good times.

I just kept on running, but with a smile on my face. I ran inside the communal toilets, pleased to find there was no one else there. I wouldn't have to explain. I swept all the hopping crickets out of the urinal trough onto the floor. "It's not your fault you were hatched in a prison," I told them.

My urine splashed into the trough, steaming and smelling of salt. I was proud of myself.

I never again peed on a cricket.

Chapter
28

*O*nce again, I turn on my laptop, planning to describe for my kids my confession to Mama. Marly sleeps next to my chair, his head resting on my feet. What a great dog he's turned out to be. I must remember to send a donation to the animal shelter.

"How long do they keep us here? It is like hell on earth and I do not apologize for the language." Mama pushed the sun-faded curtain aside and gazed forlornly out the window. "How can people live in this terrible place? Not even one tree."

I remember standing behind her with my hands touching her cheeks as she had done for me so many times before. "Your morning glories are beautiful, Mama. Someday you will have a garden again. We can plant carrots and beans. Whatever you want."

She reached up to take my hands in hers. "Forgive me, darling boy," she said. "I do just like poor Claire's mother, so sad, but, oh, we lost so many things. They are only things, because we are together. Still, they were all that I had of my mother and grandmother. The precious baby clothes Oma made for you."

Oma!

The time to tell her about giving Claire Oma's ring was here. "I have to tell you something, Mama. It's kind of bad, in a way, but I think I had a good reason. I hope you won't be mad at me."

Mama turned to face me, her expression tender and loving. I can still picture her dear face as it was that day. "You are my good boy. You would never do anything truly bad."

Believe me, I could think of a few things I'd done I was glad she didn't know about, but probably none of them was actually "bad" enough to get me in serious trouble. Standards were different in those days. "Mrs. Bienenmald was always calling me a bad boy. A bad Kraut boy. I called her a witch. Not to her face."

"Witch?" A smile tugged at the corners of Mama's mouth. "Phhhh. She is a pathetic soul who minds everybody's business but her own. She needs something to do besides torment her poor husband." To my absolute delight Mama threw her arms around me and giggled against my chest. "What kind of woman starches her husband's undershorts?"

I rested my head against Mama's hair. "A crazy one."

Mama stood up. "Shall we go to the dining hall for some tea? Then you can tell me about this terrible sin of yours."

The sun smacked me in the face like a sheet of fire. I went back for my hat, by then little more than a rag with a brim. "I wish we could make tea in our own house, like in the olden days. And strudel."

"I, too, Carl. I, too."

In the distance I could see the pair of guards on horseback, making their rounds, their rifles slung over their shoulders. The dry earth stirred under the horses' hooves and swirled into dust devils. If only some rain would come, I thought. Just to give Mama some hope.

We took the long way around, past a garden tended by a few Japanese internees, to avoid a group of thugs, true Nazis, or so they claimed. For some reason I still don't understand, these men were allowed to hold meetings and to sing their Nazi songs.

As we approached the dining hall Kenny Murakami's grandfather wandered out from behind the building, waving his hands in the air. He was dressed all in old clothes, gray from the dirty wash water, now too big for his thin body. On his head he wore a dusty baseball cap.

"Poor fellow," Mama said. "They say he doesn't even know his name or where he is. Such a danger to the United States is this man. He might show the Japanese navy how to land on California with his flashlight blinking messages from the shore."

"They used to be rich," I said.

"We were rich, too," Mama said. "Rich in all the important things."

Mr. Murakami stopped and stared at us. He pointed his fingers at the sun, smiled at me, and shrugged. *"Atsui, desu-ne, Kah-ru."*

"Konnichi-wa, Mr. Murakami," I called out, showing off a little for Mama. "That's 'hello' in Japanese. Kenny taught me." Mama placed a comforting arm across my shoulders. "I taught him some German words."

"No bad words, I hope," Mama teased.

"How would I know bad words?" Of course I did know a few from when I used to go to the German Music Society meetings in New Jersey with Papa and some of us boys traded information. How proud I had been to see Papa play his violin with the other musicians. He had not touched his violin in months even though members of the camp orchestra regularly invited him to join them.

"All boys know some," Mama said. "But when they are men, truly men, they forget about those words. At least they do not say them in front of women and children. You remember that when you are grown."

Well, I've tried to, kids, but I have probably slipped a few times!

Anyway, we climbed the steps to the dining hall. Inside was stuffy and scarcely cooler than outside, but at least the sun did not beat down upon us.

In the kitchen, a few people were chopping vegetables from the camp garden. They nodded to us, but kept working.

With a cup of tea and a bit of spice cake apiece, we sat across from one another at one of the long tables. "So, what is this thing you have done that makes your face red?"

I took a quick bite of the cake. It was like chewing on shredded wheat right out of the package. "Remember when that FBI guy was in your room the first time, and throwing everything around?"

"How can I not remember that day?" She closed her eyes and clasped a hand to her forehead.

I almost lost my nerve, seeing how bad she felt. "He pushed everything off the top of the dresser onto the floor, even Oma's ring. I picked it up and stuck it in my pocket because I thought he might steal it. Like they stole our house."

Mama nodded, her expression approving and hopeful. "Good for you. That is nothing bad. But then you left it at the house?"

Moment of truth. I took a deep breath. "No, Mama. I gave it to Claire."

"To Claire?" Mama folded her hands and looked at me in puzzlement. "So what did you tell her? We did not then know they would do this thing to us."

I could feel my face grow red again. "I didn't tell her about the FBI guys. I just told her we were engaged."

A smile broke on Mama's face. "What did Claire say?"

"She said she didn't know how to cook."

Mama smiled. "Now she does. I taught her. And she has my cookbook. Oh, Carl, what a joke that I left it for her. What must she think?" Her laughter rang in the dusty air. The more she tried to stop, the harder she laughed. Her shoulders shook and tears streamed down her face. Soon I was smiling too, laughing even, though not as hard because I had taken the engagement somewhat seriously. Finally Mama wiped her tears away with her fingertips. "I did not expect to be a mother-in-law when I am only thirty. Will I soon be a grandmother then?"

"Mama." Can you imagine how embarrassed I was?

I didn't exactly know how babies were made, but I knew both people had to be near each other with their clothes off and Claire was far away. Besides, thinking about Claire with her clothes off made me feel funny in the belly.

Okay. Strike that last paragraph. Hit the delete button. The kids would be even more embarrassed than I am at this revelation. There is a reason for the generation gap.

Just then I heard a loud bang. And another.

"Guns!" I jumped up, almost falling over the bench in my haste to get to the door. I jerked it open and looked out. In the distance, near the barbed wire fence I saw the two guards, still on horseback, pointing their rifles at the ground. A figure lay in the dust, not moving.

"My God," Mama cried. "What is wrong with those people? Who did they shoot? Why?"

I didn't have to go closer. I knew whom the guards had shot. An old man who did not know his name or where he was. "I think it's Kenny's grandfather." I bit my lip to stop the tears. "Maybe I should go to Kenny's house to tell him."

Mama grabbed me by the shoulders. "No. There is nothing you can do for that poor man, and much that those men can do to you. Please, stay with me, Carl. You can go to your friend later. We will all go."

* * *

Mr. Murakami was buried that same day, in the evening, not far from where he had been gunned down. My parents and I went to pay our respects. Kenny's family, dressed in white, looked as if they had been carved out of wood. Kenny looked up and blinked at me, but otherwise made no other acknowledgment of my presence.

I had no idea what the Japanese way of funerals was. With Mama's permission I had brought a bit of morning glory vine. I laid it on the dirt. The flowers had closed up for the night but the delicate blue of their petals provided a touch of color.

As we headed back to our quarters no one spoke. What we had seen no child, no one, should ever have to witness. I promised myself I would never speak of this time again to anyone.

Ever.

And I never have.

Well, until now.

Chapter 29

O kay, I'm back and, I apologize, but I'm going into lecture mode here. I took some time off from this free-form tirade because I had a letter to write. A U.S. Senator gave a speech a few weeks ago about the treatment of political detainees in a facility off the mainland U.S. He pleaded for humane treatment for those people. He pleaded that this country live by the principles established by those folks who fought for our freedom over two hundred years ago. He mentioned the abrogation of human rights which led to the internment of 110,000 Japanese/Americans during World War II. He failed to mention the 10,000 German Americans and approximately the same number of Italian Americans. I wrote to tell him about his oversight, in case he did not know. I am still awaiting his response. I will write to him every week until he acknowledges my message.

Your grandparents signed the paper promising never to reveal what happened to us on pain of imprisonment or deportation. (Did war-ravaged Germany ever say they *wanted* us?) My parents never uttered one word to anyone about our years of internment.

I believe in humane treatment for all people, myself included. Where is my apology? Where is the pittance of restitution owed me? Where? It is too late for my parents. They are gone. No amount of money will make up for what was taken from them — their home, their lives, their dignity. No amount of money could restore the homes and businesses lost or give back the years Kenny Murakami's grandfather might have lived. Some gesture has to be made, some acknowledgment of what was needlessly suffered.

And still today, this country takes the high moral ground with other countries about human rights, while ignoring its own precepts, when it suits, just as it did back then.

A kid I knew in camp, Johnny Coldbrook, and his parents, got sent to Germany in 1944, in exchange for Americans held by the Germans. Originally the family name was Kaltenbach, but his parents wanted to be Americans so they changed the name to an English version of the name when they became citizens. By a fluke, Johnny and I ran into each other years later. We were both in the service. In the service of THIS COUNTRY, a country that, by the way, I love dearly despite all that I have told you. It is not with the United States or its people that I have issues, but with the power-mad individuals who shame this country with their amorality and greed.

Johnny told me he only knew a few words of German when they were shipped over. He and his parents made their way to his mother's cousin's place, on foot, under enemy (i.e., U.S.) fire. The cousins had little food; their house was half destroyed. They lived in their basement. Johnny and his parents had nothing but the clothes they wore. Naturally the cousins were less than thrilled to see the "Americans," but they did what they could. Eventually Johnny made his way back to the States. His disheartened parents stayed in Germany. Do you blame them?

Kids, a great many people gave their lives so that you could have life, liberty, and the pursuit of happiness, so that you could vote! So don't forget to vote. And remember, protest is patriotic and the price of freedom is vigilance.

End of lecture. End of saga. Like Candide, it is time I cultivate my garden. However....

As you must have guessed, I'm still pretty damned mad after all these years. They continued to consider us enemy aliens, despite my American citizenship, until long after the war ended. Few people probably know or care that Truman decided that whoever was still interned at the end of the war must still be dangerous. They let the Japanese Americans go, but my parents and I were not released until 1947. Two goddam years after the war ended.

We ended up in a small town in the coal mining area of eastern Pennsylvania where one of the other internees had family and offered us a place to stay until we could get on our feet. My father, a chemist mind you, worked stocking shelves in a grocery store. Mama did her best, but her health had been compromised during the six years of internment. She never again planted a garden. All of my gardens have been my tribute to this beautiful woman.

Don't think I focus on this all the time. I cannot, will not, let it consume me twenty-four seven, as they say these days. Nonetheless, I lost my childhood, my home, my things, and to some extent my beloved parents during that awful time. War stole my friend Claire's childhood, too, as she took over a household at age eight for a mother too fragile to deal with a third child and war.

I wish now that I had filed a complaint with all those folks who did this to my family and to so many others, but they're all dead and I was still prisoner to shame. I don't believe for one second that they've gone on to some other plane of existence where they'll repent. They're just gone.

All this time I didn't want you to know what those years were like. Because I bought in to the shame, shame on *me*! This process has been hard because I was brought up to keep my negative feelings to myself. Why talk about something if you can't do anything about it?

Your mother claims that talking about something *is* doing something, if only dumping the pain out so that it doesn't give you a heart attack. Could be. By the way, I got a clean bill of health from Dr. Leventhal the other day. She claims I'll live to one hundred if I behave myself.

I bless your mother every day for teaching me, over many decades, to show my feelings, both for her and for you...in ways that can be recognized. Love, she reminds me as often as I need to hear it, is a verb, not "a purple bullfinch in the lilac tree."

So, kids, that's as much of my story I'm going to share. The telling has kind of worn me out. However, feel free to tell people about this. It happened and we should never be afraid to shout

truth from the mountaintops.
   I love you all more than you know. Dad

Chapter
30

My garden is coming along. It's the fashion now to "mass" vegetables and flowers in freeform beds rather than make the neat little soldier-like rows Mama loved. They don't even segregate edibles from non-edibles, although apparently the line between them has blurred. I find it harder to weed this new type of garden, but I like the global implications—-we're all in this together--and I'm even beginning to appreciate the effect.

Now that my tomatoes are in, I'm thinking about taking a drive toward the shore. To Marlsburg. I'll have to clean up. Deda's at an all-day quilting event in Princeton or I'd ask her to go along. I'll give her a call and let her know. Ever since my heart episode, we've both carried cell phones.

* * *

Funny. I haven't been here since I was twenty, but I find Atlantic Lane without a hitch. I remember parking in front of my old house on that fall day in 1952, looking for what I couldn't say. My young self, I guess. The grape arbor had gone wild; a haphazard garden of what looked mostly like volunteers grew in the back yard. At first the owners thought I was some door to door salesman, but they finally were convinced I was just someone who wanted to take a nostalgic trip through the back yard. I must have spent half an hour on the porch, remembering my mother with her apron thrown over her head, after the FBI guys' second visit, wishing I could comfort that young woman in my now grown-up arms.

I had hoped to find Claire, or at least her parents and maybe Stephen, still living on Atlantic Lane. The frazzled woman who answered the door to their house, with a half dozen kids hanging onto her skirts, had only lived there for two years and had no idea who the Walters family was. They had bought from somebody named de Cicco.

I decided to ask another of the neighbors if they had any information, but both Merinos had died; Dr. Rosenthal, who had served as a medic, was killed in the war; the Brownes, the Larimers, and the Franks had all moved away. Ironically the only people left from pre-war times were the Bienenmalds.

Why not knock on the old bat's door to ask if she knew where Claire's family had moved to? As I approached the house my knees trembled and I was seized by the urge to run, but the shadow I cast in my navy uniform was tall and broad. Oh, yeah, dummy. You're six feet two and half, two hundred and three pounds. She can't hurt you any more.

The door curtain was pulled aside. I recognized her immediately. She looked exactly the same except her hair, instead of shoe polish brown, was blue. She opened the door as far as the chain permitted.

"What do you want?" Her voice was shaky.

"I'm looking for Claire Walters. I know they've moved, but I hoped you might know where."

"How would I know that?" she snapped. "They've been gone for years."

"Well, you've lived here for a long time. You used to take care of her little brother. I thought maybe you exchanged Christmas cards, or something."

The scene was Disney-esque, but without the orchestra. I could almost read her thoughts in bubbles above her head. "You're... you're...." She clutched at her throat; her face went white.

I couldn't resist. "Kraut boy, Mrs. Bienenmald, back from internment camp. Did you hope they'd killed us?" Of course, by giving in to that childish urge, I ensured that even if she had their address, she wouldn't give it to me.

"Get out of here before I call the police," she croaked and slammed the door shut. I heard the clack of the bolt. At least now

I knew for sure.

The searing memory of my parents' shame and deprivation shot through me. I rapped on the glass with my class ring. "How do you live with yourself?"

And now, here I am back again, fifty-odd years later. *La Bienenmald* will be long gone, probably frozen into one of the rings of hell. I park in front of my old house. I get out and stand on the sidewalk, staring. What a weird shade of blue they've painted it. These people are either color blind or seriously anti-social.

"Hi." A small child wearing an embroidered red Mexican dress complete with comb and mantilla looks up at me. A slash of red lipstick approximates the shape of her mouth.

"Hi, yourself."

"They're on vacation."

"Who's on vacation?"

"The Porters. McKenzie's my best friend. That's her room up there." She points to the window of my old room. A flush of sorrow surges through me. Why had I come?

"Well, maybe they'll be back soon." I start to leave.

"Do you want to look in the back yard, too?"

I turn around, puzzled. "Too?"

"Yeah. Some old lady came last week. She wanted to look in the back yard. She said her best friend from when she was a little kid used to live here. She lived across the street in that house." She points at the Walters' house.

My head swims. Claire? My god, could it be? And it was...last week? I missed her by a week. "Did she tell you her name?"

The child shakes her head. "No. Just her granddaughter did. Phoebe." She squints through her fingers at me. "My name's Madison. What's yours?"

"Carl. Carl Goehner." I feel like I'm having another heart attack, but I know it's my nerves. "I used to live in this house, sixty-five years ago. My room was the same one your friend has now."

"You must be old," she says.

"I guess I am."

"Phoebe said they might come back some time." The girl twirls on one foot, holding out the ruffles of her dress.

I fumble for my wallet and pull out a card. "If they come back, will you give this to them, please?"

She takes the card and looks at it for a time. "You're a doctor?"

"Professor. Geology. I'm retired now."

She scratches at a scab on her elbow and flicks it into the grass. "Mosquito bite." She rolls her eyes. "I hate mosquitoes."

"You must be delicious." With eleven granddaughters, I have a sense of how to tease little girls.

She thinks about that for a minute and then giggles. "They went to see my Aunt Claire."

Aunt Claire? I shiver in the hot sun. "What's your aunt's last name?"

"Nishida. Same as me."

I feel myself grin ear to ear. "We used to buy fruit from a Mr. Nishida sometimes."

"So did that old lady," Madison says.

It's my Claire for sure. "My mother had a garden behind this house, but no fruit trees. Mr. Nishida had delicious peaches. Does your aunt live nearby?"

Madison points in the direction of the school. "Down that way. It's kind of far, but that lady said she knew where it was."

"So do I." I thank the girl and get in my car. I remember exactly where the Nishida house is. I can look at my old back yard some other time.

Chapter
31

❝Grandmother!" Phoebe shakes me gently. I peer at the bedside clock. I've been asleep for more than two hours.

I am a little muzzy-headed. "I didn't mean to doze off."

She sits beside me on the bed. "I guess you didn't hear the phone ring."

"Oh, I heard it. I was just too indolent to get up."

"I could kick myself," she says, looking apologetic. "I should have brought the cordless back upstairs."

I stretch and smile. "I was having a dream fantasy about my new house and my flowers and where I was going to put the kitchen." Suddenly I am scared. I sit bolt upright. "Is something wrong? Is it Mother?"

She jumps to her feet. "It's nothing bad, but I think you'll want to listen to the message on your machine." She looks solemn and excited at the same time. "Come on. I already put water on for the celebratory tea."

Celebratory. "I like the sound of that. Hint?"

"I don't want to spoil it." She grins and stands waiting, arms akimbo, head tilted to one side.

I swing my feet to the floor and feel around for my old slippers. Ringo grumbles and gets to his feet. The three of us make our way down the stairs. I grip the railing because I'm still not fully awake.

Phoebe gestures toward a chair that she has placed near the answering machine. "Sit, please."

"Maybe you should switch majors, Phoebe. To drama." I lower myself to the chair.

"This is drama all right, but I'll stick with history." Phoebe pushes the play button. "Ta dah!"

A man's voice, a voice I don't recognize, says, "Hello, Claire. This is Carl. Carl Goehner."

My mouth falls open.

"I got your phone number from Claire Nishida. I can't believe I've finally found you after all these years. You probably have my number on your Caller I.D., but just in case, here it is again. Please call me. I can't wait to talk to you."

Can it be! Carl. I cover my face with my hands. Tears stream between my fingers. So he didn't die in some prison, as Mrs. Bienenmald tried to make us think. He's not only alive, but he sounds vigorous, healthy, confident, like someone who has done well for himself in life.

"Mop up, Grandmother." Phoebe presses a tissue into my hand and I remember Mrs. Bell, so many years ago, saying the same thing, the day Mrs. Bienenmald dragged me to school by the ear. Mop up. Funny, isn't it? I am still angry about the way that woman treated me.

I press the tissue to my eyes to stanch the gush of tears. I feel a pang of deep loss mingled with a bubble of joy. Finally I look up at Phoebe through soggy eyelashes and smile. "If we hadn't gone to visit my old house, and if we hadn't gone to Carl's house, and if that little good fairy, Madison, hadn't been outside...."

"Meant to be," Phoebe says, clicking on the cordless. "Here. Dial. Or shall I?"

I am too flustered. "You do it."

She dials the number and hands me the phone. My heart is beating crazily. My throat constricts. I try to swallow.

Phoebe mouths, "I'll make the tea." She heads for the kitchen.

"Hello?" It is a woman's voice.

"This is Claire Walters Hanneman, returning Carl's call." My voice sounds almost like a little girl's. I *feel* like a little girl in a way.

"Oh, Claire, hello! How wonderful. This is Edith, Carl's wife. Hang on. I'll go get him." I hear her call him in a warm, happy voice. "Carl. Come quick. It's Claire."

I hear the click of a ring on the phone as it changes hands. A long silence precedes Carl's first words. When he speaks he sounds as if he is choking. "So here we are, finally, after too many years. I want to hear about all of them."

"My granddaughter and I were in your back yard last week." I am babbling.

"Yes, that's how I found you," he says. "That funny little girl, Madison, who lives next door to my old house, told me. She said you went to visit her great aunt."

"Mr. Nishida's daughter. She and I had a wonderful visit."

"She and I also had a nice visit. She gave me your phone number. I can't believe I missed you by only a few days. Something told me to go to Marlsburg. I guess it's what old people do. Visit their childhood home. Try to remember their young self or something."

"Your back yard's all changed. Your mother's garden is gone. I felt so sad for her. Remember how she used to wear that big floppy straw hat when she was weeding? I would never have made it through that summer without her."

"She's been gone a long time, Claire. Too long."

"I'm so sorry to hear that." Phoebe sets a mug of tea on the table. "I never thought I'd know if you were okay. I always wondered what happened to you, why you disappeared overnight. Dick and I went over to your house and the milk was still outside, in the hot sun. I was going to ask your mother to take care of Stevie while I was in school, instead of Mrs. Bienenmald, but you were gone."

"I bet she had a lot to say after we were gone."

"I never listened to her again after that. If she tried to speak to me, I put my fingers in my ears."

He chuckles. "Good." A pause. "How about your parents?"

"Dad's gone. My mother's still living."

"How is she?"

"Forgetful. Cranky. Ninety-five."

"Mama died at age forty-seven. My dad lasted one more year without her."

So young. "I've thought about you so many times over the years and wondered if you were all right. What *did* happen?"

A leaden silence follows. "Can that wait until we can talk face to face? I have something to show you."

Whatever happened to the Goehners must have been bad if he doesn't want to speak of it over the phone. "Of course. Let's not wait too long. We're pretty old, you and I!"

"Yes, and I had a serious heart attack last fall. I'm doing well now, but you never know. When will you be back this way? Claire Nishida told me you're going to build a house nearby, so I'm hoping it won't be too long. We have so much to catch up on."

"I'll change my plans and leave here in a few days."

"That would be great. You're alone now, I take it?"

"My husband died two years ago. This house is too big for one. My children are grown." I laugh. "My *grand*children are grown. I want to be near Dick, he's in a suburb of Philadelphia, and I guess I feel I ought to be near my mother. So I'm putting this house on the market, tomorrow, and starting to plan my new house."

"I remember you wanted to be an architect."

"Well, that never happened, but my granddaughter has convinced me I could design a small house for myself. I'm eager to try."

"Claire," he says, "I can't wait to see you."

"I can't wait to see you. You must be within driving distance of Marlsburg."

"We live near Princeton, just a couple of hours from there. I gather you live in New Hampshire."

"I've been here forty years." I sip my tea. I blow Phoebe a kiss.

"Plan to spend the night. Edith is looking forward to meeting you. She's almost as excited as I am."

We exchange e-mail addresses so he can send directions to his house. After I hang up I realize I forgot to tell him about his mother's cookbook and the ring. I imagine myself handing those

190

things to him.

Phoebe smiles at me. "That was the coolest thing ever."

"It is," I agree, "the coolest thing ever."

And the saddest.

What does Carl have to show me? How can I stand to wait?

Chapter
32

I am up just as the sun touches the eastern sky with pink. Claire will be here later this morning. Even though we've been exchanging e-mails for the past five days, I still can't quite believe we will meet after all these years.

I shower, shave, dress, fill a mug with coffee. Marly and I head out to the back yard. He starts off on his morning rounds as I lower myself onto the squeaky wooden swing. I'd oil it, but Deda claims to like the sound. She says it reminds her of the porch swing at her grandparents' farm.

So many memories bombard my mind as I sip my coffee. Endless red Kool-Aid in cheese glasses, drunk while playing Sorry or Chinese checkers. Watching Claire pet Mr. Nishida's horse from my bedroom window. Claire standing on a stool in her kitchen, washing dishes, while her mother slept upstairs. Claire sitting on the front steps, reading, waiting for me to come over.

What will she be like? Will I see anything of the girl I'm not sure I exactly remember? Will she be fat? Thin? Tall? Will she walk with a cane? Will she be gray-haired, or a dyed redhead, the way so many old ladies do these days? Will I recognize anything?

Will *she*? I was nine the last time she saw me, and weighed about eighty-five pounds.

I rock carefully in the swing so as not to slop coffee on my pants, admiring my yard. The lawn is thick and green, mowed three days ago so as not to appear scalped for Claire's visit. My flowers present a riot of color. Claire liked bachelor's buttons, I remember. I'm glad I planted some this year. I don't always. My vegetables seem almost gaudy...scallions by the dozen, tomato plants covered with yellow flowers and tiny green tomatoes, four kinds of lettuce, baby eggplants, foot-high corn. My carrots shake their feathery tops in the morning breeze. Deda will build a salad for our lunch with whatever can be harvested and fill in with stuff she bought at the store.

Reflecting on my life, I edit what I will share with Claire. Except for the black period I've kept hidden, I've lived well, with a dear friend for a wife, four great kids, and a gaggle of grandchildren no one would be ashamed of. Teaching and writing filled out the rest of my life in a good way.

If only...but I don't want to get into that. Why even try to imagine how our lives might have turned but for this action, or that circumstance? What if doctors had known how to help Mrs. Walters? Or if the FBI had even thought to question the lies of a stupid woman?

I see that my mug is empty. As I get up to go inside for a refill, Deda calls me. "Carl. Breakfast is ready."

I look at my watch. Seven o'clock. Claire will be here by ten. I hurry inside.

* * *

At nine forty-five, a red Jeep pulls into our driveway. Deda walks to the front window.

"She drives a Jeep?" Amusement warms her voice.

I join her to look out. "I guess so, if that's Claire."

We watch a tall, slender woman step out of the Jeep. A black and white dog jumps down and runs in circles, clearly delighted to be out of the car. Claire reaches into the Jeep and takes out a box, then starts toward the house.

Deda gives me a little push and we rush to open the front door and stand on the stoop. Marly bursts ahead and barks at the intruders, one of whom could have been a litter mate. While the dogs work things out, Claire sets down her package and runs to embrace me. We hug one another, hard, both of us suddenly in tears. After a minute or two, she pulls away and takes my face in her hands.

"You still look the same, my friend." She smiles. "And very

different."

"I wasn't sure I'd recognize you," I say, "but I do. You look like your dad."

We grin like idiots.

I turn to Deda. "This is my wife, Edith."

The two women study one another. They are both tall and slim, with white hair and blue eyes. They both wear tan jeans and blue shirts. They extend hands to shake, then hug instead, both weeping.

"Carl has talked about you all the years I've known him," Deda says. "I'm so glad to finally meet you."

"And I you. I hope it was all right to bring my dog. Ringo pretty much goes with me everywhere now that I'm alone."

Deda smiles. "They seem to be getting along just fine."

The dogs are running around, chasing each other playfully, as if they'd been friends for years.

"The back yard is fenced. Let's take them there," I say, glad to find a safe topic. Enough with the waterworks. I know there will be more, but I'd like to postpone them.

Claire turns to retrieve her package. She follows us through the house and out to the screened porch where she sets the box on the floor. I herd the dogs into the back and we all sit down. Deda had already put out a pitcher of iced tea minutes before Claire arrived. She fills glasses while I study Claire and Claire looks out at my yard.

"What a lovely garden," she says. "You must have inherited your mother's green thumb."

"She could grow anything anywhere." Even south Texas. But I need to stay on safe ground a little longer. "What do you have there?" I ask.

Grinning, Claire looks like a kid at Christmas even though she's the one bearing gifts. "Do you remember this? Of course you do." She hands me a rocket model. How dated it looks. "Steve's had it all these years. I nagged him into giving it to me to bring to you. You never really explained why you gave it to him."

I hold the model in my hands, choking. I run my fingers over the decals Papa helped me put on. My father touched this. I can't say anything.

"There's more." Claire must see what a mess I am. She hands me Mama's cookbook.

"You found it after all," Deda says.

"Yes. And a letter to Carl's mother from a relative in Munich. Link, my husband, and I went there about twenty-five years ago and tried to find the people whose name was on the envelope. I hoped to find out what happened to you, but there was someone else living in the house, someone who never heard of your mother's family."

"I tried to find you, too, in Marlsburg. I was going to ask for your forwarding address from Mrs. Bienenmald, but ended up scaring the hell out of her instead, which turned out to be fun," I tell her. "I was twenty, but she recognized me all right. She threatened to call the police if I didn't leave." I smile at the memory.

"She had something to do with what happened to you, didn't she?" Claire's face turns somber, sympathetic, sad.

I nod. "I believe so." I exchange a look with Deda for courage. "What else do you have in your bag of tricks?"

Claire hands me a pair of photographs. "First day of school. Third grade. You, me, Dick. Here's one of your parents. I found it when I cleaned out Mother's house. I think it was taken at a neighborhood party. They're copies, for you to keep."

No photographs of my family's Atlantic Lane years remain. We left them in the house, sure we would be back someday. Sure it was some terrible mistake. How young my parents look. Younger than my children are now. How skinny we kids were. What a treasure these photographs are. I nod again.

"Thank you," Deda says for me.

"Okay, Carl," Claire says with a watery smile. "I guess it's Dear John time."

Deda looks surprised, but I know what's coming. "Oma's ring." With a surge of anger I picture the FBI man sweeping Mama's things to the floor, anger at my child's helplessness, rage at my father's shame. Then I remember the time I confessed to my mother what I had done with the ring and how she laughed. It was one of the few bright spots from all those long days in the camp.

"I'm going to have to break our engagement, Carl. I think you should know I was married for fifty years to someone else." Claire places the ring gently in my hand. "I've never worn it. It was too big when you gave it me, and now I can't get it over my knuckles. I've always hoped I'd have the opportunity to return it to you. I knew it didn't come from the Penny Arcade."

A rusty chuckle escapes my lips. "I didn't think I fooled you, but thanks for pretending. At least it wasn't lost."

"The Universe stepped in and made it happen," Deda says.

Oma's ring. My body buzzes with emotion. "Yes, well the Universe was off by a week," I joke, still trying to keep things light.

"There's bound to be a little slippage in fifteen billion years," Claire quips. "Enter Madison." I suspect she's trying to keep things light, too.

"What did you think of the color of my old house?" I ask.

"Claire Nishida told me the woman's an artist. Apparently she changes the color every other year. We missed the tangerine and aqua by only a few months."

I shake my head. "I didn't much like that blue, but it helped me get over feeling that it was *my* house."

"I've always wondered how they got the money to you for the house and car and things. I wrote two letters to President Roosevelt asking about your family. All I got was a form letter thanking me for my interest in the democratic process." She rolls her eyes. "I guess he was busy with other things."

"Busy," I grumble. "Busybody. Rich phony. We never saw a penny."

Claire blinks, purses her lips. "Nothing!"

"Sore subject," Deda says. "Carl, it's time to get your gift for Claire."

I don't want to give it to her. And I do. I put off the moment.

"I wrote you a letter once, but the censors cut out so much I never sent it." I hurry from the room before the rage turns my face purple.

"Censors?" Claire cries.

I don't wait to hear Deda's reply.

Chapter
33

❝Censors?" I nearly choke.

Carl's wife reaches toward me and takes my hand. "He's kept it bottled up all these years. Even the kids didn't know until a few months ago. I was the only other person who knew and I had to practically extort it from him." She lets go of my hand. "After his heart attack last fall I convinced him that he had to share what happened to him and his parents with his children, that he needed to exorcise those demons if he wanted to live, that it was the government's shame, not his. I've tried to get him to open up for years, but until he had that health scare, he wasn't ready to listen." Her face softens. "He's a good man. I didn't want to lose him."

I blink back tears. "I knew it had to be something big." This is going to be tough. Sensing that she's not going to tell me anything more, I wait quietly for Carl's return.

He stands in the doorway looking at his wife, then at me. His face is pale, with bright spots of red on his cheeks. "Well, here's the magnum opus. The war years according to Carl Goehner." He hands me a slim manuscript, bound in blue. The title is printed on a red-trimmed white tag. "Loyal German Americans Interned for the Duration."

"Interned?" I blurt. "I thought it was only the Japanese Americans."

"A lot more of them than us, but many German and Italian Americans. I think you'll find answers to most of your questions. Maybe, after lunch, you'd like to read it."

I nod, unable to manage more than, "Oh, yes."

Epilogue

Ringo and I are moving a little slower these days, a year after moving into my wonderful little Japanese inspired house that overlooks the bay. Claire Nishida, driving her high-tech van, visits frequently and always clasps her hands with delight when she comes inside, declaring that I should have been an architect. Sometimes Madison comes with her.

Mother died in her sleep soon after I left New Hampshire. We never had that conversation, but I've let that go. I tell myself she did her best with what she had at the time. Sometimes I almost even believe it.

Now that Phoebe has graduated from CSU, she and Brad, the solstice shrub guy, are doing a world tour on a shoestring. No marriage plans so far, but that may come. If not, well, they will have had a grand time together.

Life is not something you can model, like clay, or build like a rocket. You just hang on and try to help one another.

Oh, yes. Carl's book broke my heart a dozen times, especially learning how he had tried to find me. Once he'd finally told his story, Carl caught fire with the need to pass it on. Since our first meeting he and Edith have traveled to the places where he and his parents were interned. They've taken hundreds of pictures with the digital camera his kids gave him at Christmas. A university press will publish "For the Duration" in the spring.

I can't help thinking it would make a great movie.